Mail Order Muse

Book Fifty in the Brides of Beckha

Kirsten Osbourne

Unlimited Dreams Publishing

Cover design by Erin Dameron Hill/ EDH Graphics

Visit my website at www.kirstenandmorganna.com

Chapter One

After finishing her morning walk, Keri Bateman stopped to get the mail, expecting good news from her publisher. Keri had written her debut book at eighteen, which changed her life. She had been able to move out of her childhood home and rent a small house in Beckham, Massachusetts, which was near the farm where she'd grown up.

Her first book was about the pitfalls of being the eldest child in a family of fourteen children. She'd written it as a school project, and when her teacher had suggested she send it to a publisher, she had done so immediately.

The book was filled with humor, personal stories, and a grand love at the end. The boy she'd felt she loved, who she'd modeled the character after, had married her younger sister soon after the book had been published.

She'd spent the past four years, trying to recreate the success of her first piece with no success and a rapidly depleting bank account. If this newest book didn't sell, she'd have to move right back in with her family, and she knew she'd never write another book living there. Her family was loud and rowdy, and they were not conducive to the silence she needed to put her words on paper.

When the postmistress handed her the letter she'd been waiting for, she said, "Oh, thank you so much," and then she stepped outside the post office to sit on a bench that was situated just outside. There, she opened the letter and read it.

"We regret to inform you..."

She didn't continue reading. There was no reason why she would. Her past five books had been declined. Taking a deep breath, she blinked a few times to hold back the tears that threatened to fall. She could not move back in with her family. She would end up spending all her time cooking, cleaning, and minding her younger siblings.

She felt rather than saw someone sit beside her on the bench, and a comforting hand covered her own. Looking to see who it was, Keri spotted Mrs. Elizabeth Tandy, who though several years older than her, she'd gone to school with at one point, and she'd spent all of her schooldays with the demon horde, as Elizabeth's younger brothers and sisters had been dubbed.

"Are you all right?" Elizabeth asked.

Keri nodded. "My latest book was rejected by my publisher. Again." She shook her head. "I've gone through the money from the first book, and I'm going to have to move in with my parents and thirteen of my younger siblings."

"I see," Elizabeth said. "I do know how you feel. I'm the second of sixteen children, and well, you know what my siblings are called as well as I do."

"I do," Keri said, feeling forlorn.

"Have you thought about becoming a mail-order bride? That was the perfect solution for my sister, Susan. So perfect that I now run the mail-order bride agency that placed her in Texas."

Keri thought about that for a moment. "How long does that take? I have four months of expenses left." Even if she'd gotten the book deal, she'd have been very pressed financially for a few months.

"It will be much faster than that," Elizabeth promised. "I have a man in Wyoming who is looking for a bride. He said to simply send him a telegram and let him know when to be at the train station. He doesn't need you to write letters or anything."

"Are children involved?" Keri asked. There was no way she'd put herself into the same situation she'd have at home.

Elizabeth shook her head. "I know better than to send you to a home filled with children. No, he's a rancher in Wyoming. He does need someone to cook and clean, but he's tidy."

Keri thought for a moment. "Can I read the letter?"

"Of course! Let me get my mail, and then we'll walk to my house together. The letter is there."

"Thank you," Keri said, not believing her good luck. She had no idea how she hadn't known there was a matchmaker for mail-order brides in town, but she was very happy to know about it.

The walk to the Tandy residence was short, and when they arrived, Elizabeth led the way back to her office. When she spotted her husband, she sent him for tea and cookies.

"Oh, I don't need refreshments," Keri said, knowing she could make something for herself at home."

"Let us treat you," Elizabeth said, smiling sweetly as she flipped through a pile of letters on her desk.

As soon as Keri's hands were on the letter she read it quickly.

Dear Mrs. Elizabeth Tandy,

I hope this letter finds you in good health and high spirits. My name is Harry, and I am a rancher in Wyoming. I have spent my life tending to my land and cattle, living a simple yet fulfilling life under the vast skies of the West.

My ranch is my pride and joy. Every fence is straight, every barn door is secure, and not a single blade of grass is out of place. But as tidy as it all is, there's a silence that echoes across this land.

In the quiet hours, I find myself yearning for companionship. Not just any companionship, mind you, but a partner—someone to share in the joys and challenges that come with life on the ranch.

I've heard about your remarkable talent for matchmaking, and it's with a hopeful heart that I write to you today. I seek a woman of strong will and gentle heart, someone who isn't afraid to get her hands dirty during the day but can appreciate the simple beauty of a western sunset in the evening.

I don't have children, and my life might seem lonely to some, but I believe that it's a life full of potential for the right person. I can offer a peaceful home, a steady life, and a partner who values respect, kindness, and a shared effort in all things. In return, I hope to find a woman who could be my companion, my confidante, and perhaps, in time, my heart's counterpart.

If you know of a lady who might find happiness in the wide-open spaces of Wyoming, who might enjoy the quiet life of a rancher's wife, and who is willing to embark on this adventure of a lifetime, I would be much obliged if you could send her my way. I only ask that you send a telegram to me when she is on her way, so I know when to wait for the train.

I eagerly await your response. Thank you for offering hope to those of us searching for love in this vast world.

Yours sincerely,

Harry White

"He makes his ranch sound like the most wonderful place on Earth!"

"Doesn't he? It sounds so quiet and peaceful. One thing I miss about my childhood was living in the country, where the only sounds you hear are those of nature and your family. Well, I'm sure you know my family was loud, but I'd wake up before dawn, just to enjoy the peace."

"I remember doing the same thing. Why have we not been friends all these years?" Keri asked, knowing she'd found a kindred spirit in Elizabeth.

Elizabeth smiled. "Probably because we were both too busy with our lives. You were writing your books, and I was sending women west to marry strangers. Where was there time? Now I'm married, and I have children, which is an additional demand on my time. I would love to write to you when you're settled and have time."

"You're assuming I'm going to marry Harry?" Keri asked.

"Aren't you?" Elizabeth's lips quirked upward in a smile.

"Yes, I'll marry him. I will need a week to pack up my house so I can have my belongings shipped to me."

Elizabeth nodded. "That sounds reasonable. It's Tuesday. Would leaving on Monday give you enough time? I like to give my grooms as much notice as possible."

"Yes, Monday would be perfect." Keri rubbed her hands together. "Now to pack up everything I own into crates."

"No, first you will have tea and cookies with me since we're going to be friends now."

Keri smiled. "I'd be delighted."

As they ate, they caught up on each other's lives. Keri was surprised to know that Elizabeth had married her butler. Elizabeth was surprised that Keri's book had done so well, but not another had been considered good enough to publish. As they chatted, they formed a real liking for one another, something that didn't happen often enough for Keri.

When she went to her solitary home, she immediately began sorting through her belongings, trying to decide what to keep and what she could sell. She had many dresses she'd purchased right after her book sold when she was certain she'd have unlimited funds for the rest of her life.

Finally, on Saturday afternoon, she requested that her belongings be shipped to Wyoming, and she spent the weekend in one of Elizabeth

Tandy's spare rooms. On Sunday, she walked out to her parents' house, a sturdy farmhouse that was much too small for the sheer number of people who lived there.

When she arrived, two of her brothers were in a fistfight in the yard, while one of her little sisters played with one of the Miller children. By playing, she meant they were sitting in a tree with a small basket full of something small they were using as a projectile to throw at passing wagons.

Keri shook her head and simply walked past it all. It was no longer her problem. When she got into the house, she called out for her mother, whom she hadn't seen in a few months. To her surprise, though she didn't know why she was surprised, her mother was huge with child. "I didn't know you were expecting again, Ma."

Her mother beamed as she patted her belly. "I think it's twins this time!"

Keri didn't try to comprehend her mother's enthusiasm about having two more babies. It made no sense to her, and she refused to even think about it. She hugged her mother. "I have news."

Ma clapped her hands together. "Another book?"

Keri shook her head, sighing. "No one wants the last few books I've written. No, I'm going to Wyoming to marry a kind man named Harry. I'm going to be a mail-order bride."

"I see. I'd suggest you move home instead, but I'm afraid there is no room. Not even for the children we have here." Ma shrugged. "You could sleep in the top of the barn if you'd help around the house."

Her ma looked as if she was being benevolent with the offer, but Keri wanted no part of it. "No, I'm going to marry Harry."

"Keri will marry Harry," Ma said. "Why does that make me want to roll around on the floor laughing?"

"I wouldn't know," Keri said, refusing to see the humor in the names. "I leave Monday on the first train."

"Monday? So soon?" Ma sighed. "I was going to ask you to watch your siblings for a couple of days so your pa and I could get away and have some peace and quiet before the babies come."

"I'm sorry, Ma. I simply can't."

"What are you doing with all of your things?" Ma asked.

"I've already shipped them ahead to Wyoming."

"I see. I would have thought you could have given some of your older dresses to your younger sisters."

"I thought about that, but I'll one day have daughters who need clothes, and I don't know what my financial situation will be when I arrive in Wyoming." Keri stood and walked into the kitchen, noting there were dirty dishes piled everywhere. She had no idea how her mother lived with such filth and chaos. "I'll clean your kitchen before I leave," she said, rolling up her sleeves and using the pump in the kitchen to fill a huge pot that she set on the stove.

"Oh, good. Thank you. I was going to get to them."

"I know, Ma." When she was pregnant, her mother cared about very little other than the baby she was carrying. It was as if nothing else in the world mattered to her at all.

It took her more than an hour, but when she left, the kitchen looked like it could be cooked in. All the dishes were done, the kitchen window was washed, and the counters and floors were scrubbed. It was truly clean. "Now have Maisie keep up with this," Keri said. "She's eighteen, out of school, and she has no job. She should be keeping the house clean."

Ma shrugged. "She was never a tidy one like you are."

Keri said a silent prayer that Harry was tidy. They'd live their life in a clean home and not something that was unfit for pigs.

When she left, she hoped she would never come back. She hadn't said goodbye to her pa, but she couldn't even remember the last time she'd spoken to him. Oh yes, when he'd come to ask her for money six months before. She'd given it to him, of course, but that was why she didn't have enough money for another year as she'd planned. But it was all right. She'd write her mother on occasion, and that would be that. She doubted any of them remembered her when she wasn't right in front of them anyway.

Back in town, she went to the Tandys' home, knowing it was the last day she would sleep in Beckham, Massachusetts. Suddenly the lonely plains of Wyoming sounded like the most wonderful place in the world to be.

She carefully put all the things she would be taking with her into her carpet bag, and she packed it for the train. There was nothing else to do, so she sat and wrote in her journal, describing the feeling of being on the precipice of adventure, and knowing that she was going to have a better life when she reached her destination.

In her mind, Harry would take one look at her and pull her into his arms. After he kissed her, he would tell her that he'd waited for her to come into his life every day since he'd started his ranch. It would be a moving scene, and everyone on the train platform would notice and applaud their love.

They would get married right there, where they'd met and shared their first kiss, and the world would be a better place, simply because she'd responded to an ad to become a mail-order bride. They would live happily ever after, and every step she took would grow flowers where her dainty foot had trod.

Even she had to giggle at the silliness. Harry was just a man, and she was just a woman. She only hoped they were able to be together and share their love for one another.

Chapter Two

When Keri finally got off the train in Wyoming, she was exhausted. She'd thought she would be able to look out the windows and write down her thoughts, documenting her entire journey, but instead, the motion of the train had made her sick to her stomach, and she had passed her journey in a blur of nausea and sleeplessness.

By the time she stood on the platform, looking around her, she wondered why she had put herself through so much.

And then she spotted him. The man that was there to make all her dreams come true. At least she thought it was him, because he was giving her curious looks. When her eyes met his, he approached. "Are you Keri?" he asked.

She nodded. "Forgive my appearance. I'm afraid the train and my stomach did not become friends during my journey."

"I'm sorry you were sick. Are you all right now?" he asked, eyeing her skeptically.

"I believe I am. Though it still feels as if the world is moving around me a bit."

"The pastor's house is just a few blocks from here. Would you do better walking or riding in my wagon?"

"Walking," she said confidently. "I definitely should be walking."

He offered her his arm, and they walked toward the pastor's house. "Were you able to keep anything in your stomach during the ride?" he asked.

She shook her head. "Nothing at all. I quit trying after the first day. I've had a few sips of water, but nothing else."

"That can't be healthful."

"I know it isn't, but I really had no choice. It was a very rough ride."

She looked puny to him, and he worried she wouldn't be up for the task of being a ranch wife.

He knocked on the door of the preacher's house, and when it opened he smiled. "We're here to see Reverend Samuels."

"Of course, Harry. Come inside."

Ten minutes later, after no fuss at all, they were married. Harry kissed her cheek, a little worried about what her breath would smell like after so much illness.

As they walked back toward the train station, and his wagon, he asked, "Could you perhaps eat a few bites at the diner here? I assure you their food is good, and from the looks of you, you're not going to make it to the ranch without something inside you."

"I think that's a wonderful idea," she said. "Do they usually serve soup?"

He nodded. "It's a different soup every day, but they almost always have one."

In the diner, he chose a table and held her chair for her. He set her carpetbag down between their chairs. "This is all you brought?" he asked.

She smiled. "I had most of my belongings shipped. We'll be deluged in a day or two."

He nodded. "I have a four-bedroom house the previous owner built, and very little for it. Your belongings will be welcomed."

"Wonderful. I was afraid I'd just clutter your house, but it sounds like that won't happen. Tell me about your ranch."

He smiled. "It's not a huge spread, but it's certainly big enough for me to profit nicely. I have ten cowhands who work with me, one of whom serves as foreman on days that I'm out of town fetching my bride from the train station. When I first started out, I was doing it all alone, but now I have enough people that my work is much lighter."

"That's nice. Do you have parties or times where I'll need to cook for a large group of people?" she asked, peering out the window at the beautiful spring day.

He shook his head. "Only at roundup, and I've always simply hired someone to cook for that. It was two weeks ago, so nothing to worry about until this time next year. You can choose to do the cooking, or I can hire someone."

"That sounds good," she said. "I think it will depend on how everything is going at the time."

"Are you sure you won't mind the silence of the prairie?"

"I'm a writer," she said. "I've had one book published, and I'd like to write more. The quiet is exactly what I need."

"Oh, really? What do you write about?"

She shrugged. "My first book was about being the oldest of fourteen children and the shenanigans my younger siblings pulled. There was a great deal of humor in it, and I made good money from it, but I haven't been able to sell anything since. Do you mind if I continue writing and trying to publish?"

"Not at all. I think it's wonderful. I would love to read the book you've published if you don't mind."

Keri smiled. "I like that idea. I have a few copies coming when my belongings arrive."

"Did you live at home until you got on the train to come to me?" he asked.

She shook her head. "No, I moved out as soon as that first book sold. The chaos of so many younger siblings made me ache for a place of my own."

"Well, I do hope writing gets easier for you."

"I'm sure it will. I just need to find my muse."

"I would think your muse would be within you, is it not?"

They both turned their attention to the waitress who had brought them water. "What will you have?"

"What's your soup today?" Keri asked.

"Vegetable beef with barley."

"That's what I want," she said. "It sounds heavenly."

Harry did not follow suit. "I'll have a steak, medium rare, a baked potato, and asparagus."

"I'll get it ready for you." The waitress walked off.

"Do you come here often?" she asked. She had no idea how remote his ranch would be, but hopefully, it would be close enough that they could come to town when they wanted.

He nodded. "Every week after church, and if I'm in town for supplies, I always come here. I make two meals, and I make them well, but I get sick of eating the same thing day after day."

She smiled at that. "What do you make?"

"Scrambled eggs with bacon. And a pot of bean soup also with bacon. I cannot for the life of me, figure out how to make anything else."

"You won't have to worry about cooking anymore. I enjoy cooking a great deal. It'll be fun to cook for someone besides myself for a change."

"Good. I like to eat a lot, but I'm not very good at making it happen. I'll probably eat at home with you most days for all three meals. I've been eating what my cowboys eat, but they never eat anything that I can't make on my own."

"We'll change that," she said, just then realizing that as she sipped her water, she had no thoughts of bringing it back up. Thank heavens. "I think water is what I needed most."

"You look a little less green around the gills," Harry said. "Good. I thought I married a sickly woman."

"I'm never sick," she said. "It was just the motion of that godawful train."

"Glad to hear it. It's only about fifteen minutes out to the ranch, and I hope that won't be long enough for you to get sick."

"It shouldn't be," Keri said. "I'm so happy to be back on a nonmoving surface I can't even express it."

He chuckled. "Sounds like you got more than you bargained for in the journey."

"Trust me, I did. I've had people tell me how wonderful train travel is, as you can just do whatever you want. I thought I'd fill notebooks about the experience while the train clattered on, but I did nothing productive at all."

"But now you're here and you don't have to worry about the journey being that rough again," he said.

"This is true." She rubbed the back of her neck as the waitress dropped off their food. "I hope you won't mind if I insist on a bath as soon as I arrive at your place. I have never in my life felt as disgusting as I feel at this moment."

He chuckled. "I have an indoor privy. You spend as long as you need. Since it's after five, this will be our supper, and I won't need you to do any cooking until morning."

"I should be mostly back to myself by then." Her soup was very pleasing. There was a heavy beef taste to the broth, and the chunks of meat were small and very tender. "This soup is delicious. Thank you for bringing me here."

"I'm glad I did," he said. "I was starting to worry that I'd made a mistake whenever I looked at that sickly woman who got off the train."

She smiled. "What do you prefer for your meals?"

He shrugged. "Beef is always welcome. So are potatoes. I would like to never eat another bean if we could manage that. I love fried chicken and pork."

"Sounds like you'll be easy to feed," she said, making mental notes. "Is there anything you would like me to not cook other than beans?"

He thought about it for a moment. "Not really. I'm not picky about what I eat."

"That will make things a great deal easier for us," she said. "Is your kitchen well-stocked, or should I think about shopping in the morning?"

"I'm well stocked. I had a friend's wife make me a list of everything I needed to have on hand, and I believe she did an exceptional job."

"Thank you. That makes it that much easier to settle in. I'm getting excited."

"You weren't before?" he asked.

"I was before I left. I had all these beautiful thoughts of how things would be here, but they were pushed down by the nausea. Now that I'm here, the beautiful thoughts are back again."

As they finished eating, he paid the waitress, and they left the establishment, headed for his wagon again. "My carpet bag?" she asked.

"It's here," he said, holding it up. As she felt better, she looked better as well. He was no longer worried that he was married to a woman who wouldn't be able to do a lick of work. That wouldn't have been at all what he wanted.

When they reached his wagon, he tossed her bag in the back and helped her up. "I'll be careful around any holes in the road," he promised.

"I would appreciate that."

He did a good job of driving and avoiding the pitfalls she worried about. Instead, the journey out to the ranch was pleasant, and there had been nothing to worry about.

As soon as they arrived at the ranch, she jumped down from the wagon without waiting for help, eager to see her new home. Her first impression was that it needed a family to fill it. Just two people weren't enough.

"May I go in?" she called, and he nodded, looking pleased she was so excited.

She found the kitchen first and looked around, noting that the pantry truly was stocked well. She lifted the handle on the floor and climbed down to the cellar to look at the different foods he had there.

When she popped her head back up, he was just bringing in her carpetbag. "If you want to get that bath, I'll be unhitching the horses, and doing the milking. You have plenty of time."

She nodded, thrilled she would be able to bathe in peace. She'd had to fill her tub at home, and here it was just a turn of a knob. She felt Wyoming was more civilized than the way she'd lived in Massachusetts.

She took a change of dress into the privy and started the water filling the bathtub. What a luxury. She couldn't wait to soak in the tub and truly get clean.

She washed her hair and every other nook and cranny of her body, wanting to be clean and acceptable to him. She used the toothbrush she'd brought with her, and she finally felt clean enough to face her new husband. Wishing she'd been clean upon meeting him was worthless, as that was over and done.

She brushed her hair dry, and pinned it up in a bun atop her head, feeling like a wife. She looked like one as far as she could tell. Hopefully, now, she could be pleasing to Harry.

She stepped out of the bathroom, and noticed her bag still on the table, wondering where she should sleep. Would he want her in bed with him immediately, or would he be happy for her to use a spare room? Either way, she wanted to settle where she would stay, so she waited for him to return from his chores, as she explored the house on her own.

There was one bedroom, the dining room, kitchen, privy, and parlor on the first floor, and upstairs, she found three more bedrooms. It would be so nice to be able to have children and have a place to put them, she thought. When her parents had discovered they were expecting, they'd always shuffled children around, trying their best to fit them all.

Thankfully, she wouldn't be raising her children in the kind of poverty she'd been brought up in.

When she went back downstairs, she found Harry standing there, as if he had no idea where she could be. "Sorry, I was exploring the house," she said. "Where should I put my carpetbag?"

"In my room," he said, his eyes traveling up and down her body. "You look much better after your bath."

"The bath, food, and water combination have made me feel like myself again. I cannot tell you how good it felt to bathe and brush my teeth after so long on the train."

"I'm sure it felt great. My bedroom is the one downstairs."

She nodded, carrying her bag into it. As much as she worried about their wedding night, she was also thrilled he wanted her in his room. Maybe the thoughts were conflicting but they made sense to her.

He followed her into the bedroom, noting she was immediately putting her things away. "We haven't discussed a wedding night..."

She nodded. "I know. I was wondering how you wanted to handle that."

He shrugged. "Honestly, I'd like to just go ahead and have it tonight if you think you're up for that."

"I think so," she said. "I'm nervous about it as any new bride would be, but I'm sure you'll be gentle and kind."

"You know what happens on a wedding night?" he asked.

"I grew up on a farm. If I didn't know, I'd be a very confused woman," she said with a smile. "Besides, my ma was always open about it. She's expecting twins again right now."

He shook his head. "I want to stop having children before we're that old," he said.

"She had me at fourteen," Keri said. "She's only thirty-eight."

"That's a lot of children in a short time."

"I think so too. I think I'd be happy with two or three children down the road. I want to get my next book published first." Keri didn't want to live off his wealth. She wanted some of her own, which only made sense. Once a woman started earning money, she never wanted to stop.

Chapter Three

Since they'd had supper in town, and the house was just as neat and tidy as Harry had promised, Keri sat down at the table to make some notes about her arrival in Wyoming. She liked the idea of writing about a woman who went west as a mail-order bride, though she wasn't certain such a thing would sell.

She would still make notes about her journey, and her relationship with Harry, and hopefully, she would learn enough to write her first fiction novel. She was certain the thing that helped her first book sell so well was the humor peppered throughout. Now if she could just repeat that type of humor in a work of fiction, she knew it would sell. She felt it deeply within her.

"Are you working on a book?" Harry asked, sitting down at the table and putting a knife to a block of wood.

"Not really. I'm simply making notes about my journey west and thinking I could possibly write a fictional story about a mail-order bride. I do think something like that would sell, as long as there was humor involved. I've realized that's what's been missing from my latest books. Humor."

"Everyone enjoys laughing," Harry said simply.

"So where did you come from?" Keri asked. "Have you always been in Wyoming?"

He shook his head. "Rhode Island. I'm a banker's son. When my father was killed in an accident, my mother remarried pretty quickly. Her new husband wasn't particularly fond of me, so I took my inheritance and followed my dreams of owning a ranch. I didn't plan to buy one with such a large house, but it just worked out that way."

"I love the house," she told him. "Especially the indoor privy."

He grinned. "That was one of the selling points for me."

"I've never lived in a house with an indoor privy. Well, I did for two days right before I left to come here, but never other than that."

"Where did you stay for two days?" he asked, raising an eyebrow.

"With Elizabeth Tandy and her family. She was the matchmaker who gave me your letter."

"Why did you stay with her?"

"I packed up my house and shipped all my belongings here," she said softly. "I didn't even have a pot to cook in, and Elizabeth offered. Does that bother you?"

He shrugged. "I guess I would have preferred you staying in a hotel, but if it worked for you..."

"It definitely did," she said. "I knew Elizabeth as a small child, but we didn't become friends until we met again a few weeks ago. That gave me just a little bit more time with her before I left."

"Are you homesick?" he asked.

She shook her head. "No, I have no real ties to Beckham other than family, and I have no desire to go back to them. My home is with you now."

"I guess it is," he said, looking down at his whittling.

"Is it a bad thing?" she asked. "Do you not like me?"

"You certainly get straight to the point, don't you?" Harry shook his head. "I like you just fine. I don't know what I expected when you got off the train, but you are not it. I just need a bit to adjust."

Keri frowned. She'd hoped he would see her and immediately be thrilled she'd answered his ad, but it didn't seem as though that was the case. "I'll do my best to be a good wife to you," she promised.

"I know you'll be a good wife. I just...I guess it's like when you're a small child, and you anticipate Christmas. All I wanted was a wooden train set, and instead, my father and I built a treehouse together, and that was my gift—the lumber for the treehouse. I had a wonderful time building with Father and playing in my treehouse, but it wasn't the train I'd wanted. Does that make any sense at all?"

"I always got an orange for Christmas."

He made a face. "An orange isn't a Christmas present. That's sad."

She smiled. "I was always so happy to get them."

"We'll have a real Christmas this year," he said. "I'll shoot a turkey, and you can make it with all the fixings. And we'll find a pine tree for the house, and we'll decorate it together. We'll string cranberries and popcorn. It'll be beautiful."

She smiled. "That sounds very nice."

"It will be. I promise." He glanced at the clock. "It's nine. I get up at five for chores. It's time for us to turn in."

Keri nodded. She'd become gradually more nervous all day, and now she felt like she was in a panic. Of course, she'd promised to be a good wife, and this was the first step. "I'll change into my nightgown. Give me five minutes," she said, closing her journal and standing up.

Harry waited at the table, his eyes on the clock. Five minutes sounded like no time at all unless you were anticipating something. And he was definitely anticipating his wedding night.

It felt like a week, but finally five minutes had passed. He walked to his bedroom and knocked on the door, which made no sense in his mind, but he was certain she was expecting it. Women were strange that way.

He opened the door to find her in the bed, covered with only her head and arms sticking out from under the covers. He turned down the lamp and stripped down to nothing, climbing into the opposite side of the bed.

"Are you nervous?" he asked.

She laughed softly. "I have never been more nervous about anything in my life."

"I'll make it as painless as possible." He reached over and pulled the covers down so she was at least accessible to him. Then he kissed her, and he put his heart and soul into the kiss. He'd kissed a few women back east, but he'd never actually made love before, but he certainly understood how it worked.

He carefully moved his hands over her, cupping her breasts through the fabric of her nightgown. They were both out of breath when he asked, "May I take this off now?"

She nodded, surprised to find herself enjoying what was happening between them. His kisses left her weak in the knees, and she was thrilled she was lying down and not standing. His hands on her breasts caused a deep ache between her thighs, and she realized her body was readying itself for his penetration.

After her nightgown was gone, he moved closer to her, and she could feel his bare body up against her. Never had she felt anything like it. Oh, how she wanted to tell him to move faster, but she felt deep down it was a mistake.

His lips went to her neck and kissed their way down to her breast. When he pulled her nipple into his mouth and suckled, she was shocked. She had been certain only babies enjoyed a woman's breast that way, but what he did sent fissures of desire through her body.

Finally, she couldn't take his teasing anymore. "I need you inside me," she whispered.

He raised his head from her breast, clearly surprised that she had said such a thing. "Are you sure?"

She nodded emphatically, and like most men, he didn't have to be asked twice. He moved to cover her body completely with his own and reached down one hand to guide himself inside her.

She gasped in pain for just a moment, and then he was there, completely inside her, making her feel full. When he didn't move, she began moving under him, hoping it would tell him she needed more than his motionless presence within her.

As he started to move, she wrapped her legs around his waist, trying to pull him in deeper. This felt so much better than her mother had told her. No wonder her parents had so many children!

His lips were on hers when he plunged into her one last time, and she felt ecstasy wash over her. Never again would she be afraid of the marriage act. It felt just as good as she'd hoped it would.

They fell asleep with her on her side facing away from him, and him wrapped all around her. She liked the idea of having a baby with him, but she hoped it would wait a while. Keri wanted to enjoy this feeling for as long as possible.

When she woke just before dawn the following morning, she rose and went into the kitchen to start breakfast. Her mind couldn't stop thinking about what they'd done the night before, and even though there was some soreness between her thighs, she couldn't wait to do it again.

She made a simple breakfast of fried eggs, bacon, and pancakes while he milked the cows and gathered eggs. When he came back inside, he took a deep sniff of the air. "That smells so good to me!"

She turned and smiled. "Does it smell as good as last night felt?" Keri knew she probably shouldn't talk about what they'd done in bed together, but she didn't care. It was her marriage, and as long as no one was listening, she felt it was just fine to talk about.

He smiled, surprised at her frank question, but not minding it one bit. "Nothing smells quite that good." He walked to her and kissed her, gripping her bottom through the fabric of her dress. "I want to do it again already."

"Will there be time after breakfast?" she asked, more than a little eager to enjoy him again.

"If we eat fast and you do the dishes after."

Keri smiled. "Sounds absolutely wonderful."

She quickly set the table and served breakfast. "I forgot to ask if you're a coffee drinker."

He nodded. "I am."

"Good. So am I!" She poured them each a cup of coffee and sat down at the table, taking his hand for their prayer.

The prayer was quick, but she'd expected that. They both ate quickly, though they tried to be mannerly about it. When they were finished a few minutes later, he took her hand and pulled her back to the bedroom. "I think I like being married," he said with a grin.

When he'd left for the day, she made a lunch to share with him, wondering if they would enjoy themselves after lunch the way they had after breakfast. Unfortunately, she could think of little else than how it felt when he moved into her body. Oh, dear. She really didn't want to have as many children as her mother had, and she knew just what caused them.

For lunch, she made fried chicken and mashed potatoes, something she'd fixed for herself often in Massachusetts. It was one of her favorite meals, and she hoped he enjoyed it just as much. The loaves of bread she was making wouldn't be ready until suppertime, and she hoped he wouldn't mind that.

She'd also scrubbed the floor in all the main areas of the house, as well as cleaned the kitchen until it looked as if it had never been used. Of course, she'd then fried chicken in it, so it no longer looked unused. Perhaps she would just scrub it while supper was cooking each evening, so it would always look perfect when Harry was home for supper.

When he came in at noon, she had lunch waiting on the table. "How was your morning?" she asked.

He shrugged. "Busy as usual. We had a few of our cattle get out and into the neighbor's pasture, but my men and I got them back. Now I'll have to have two men spend the afternoon repairing those fences."

"How much time do you have before you have to go back to work?" she asked.

He grinned. "An hour total. Are we eating fast again?"

She nodded happily. She was certainly glad he enjoyed what they did together as much as she did. Keri couldn't help but wonder how it would be if he was on his back and she could have her way with him. That would probably have to wait until the evening.

After he was back at work an hour later, she thought about just how much she was enjoying being with her new husband. She'd never heard of a book being published that talked about the joys of the marital bed, but she had a feeling her mail-order bride book would have to at least allude to how much fun could be had with a husband.

There was no land plowed to start a garden, which was what she'd wanted to do that afternoon. She would need to talk to Harry about that later. Perhaps he could hitch up one of the horses to his plow and she could plow the area she needed. It's not like she hadn't done that more times than she could count as a farmer's daughter.

She made sure all the laundry was done up, and she went through all his clothes to be certain nothing needed mending. She wasn't surprised to find several pairs of socks in need of repair, and a few shirts that needed to be either patched or turned into rags. She would give him the option.

She spent the afternoon baking and mending, putting a beef and potato pie into the oven for supper, and making a cake for their dessert. Harry got in a few minutes later than she expected him, and supper was waiting for him on the table. "I hope your afternoon was better than your morning!" she said as she put a fresh loaf of bread onto the table.

He walked to her and kissed her quickly. "Supper smells delicious."

"This is one of my favorite receipts," she told him. "Steak and potato pie, and I did a side of green beans and of course a loaf of fresh bread."

"I'd have married you just for your cooking!" he said.

She smiled. "I love cooking. It wasn't as much fun when I was just cooking for one, but now that I have someone eating the food I cook, it's a pleasure again."

He put the pail of milk he carried onto the counter before washing his hands. "The fence is fixed. The herd is moved to fresh grazing land, and life is good again."

"I think so too," she said as she fixed his plate as well as her own. Keri had never dreamed happiness would come from being married, and a mail-order bride at that. Life surprised her sometimes.

Chapter Four

Every morning once the breakfast dishes were done, Keri sat at the table and wrote in her mail-order bride story for an hour. Her heroine experienced so many things on the train and then on a stagecoach on the way to her destination. It was fun to throw every catastrophe she could come up with at the heroine, flinching as she thought what someone writing her story would have done to her.

Within her first month of being in Wyoming, she'd put in a garden, scrubbed the house from top to bottom, dealt with Harry's mending, and cooked more meals than she could count. She just had more time in her day than was needed for her chores. Things would be different when children started coming, but there were no children yet.

Harry didn't mind that she was writing. At least she didn't think he did. She'd mentioned that she was writing a silly novel about a mail-order bride, and he'd just laughed. She wasn't sure if that meant he thought it was a good thing or a bad thing, but either way, he didn't tell her to stop, and that was important to her. She wasn't certain she would have stopped because she didn't believe women should have to blindly obey their husbands, but she was glad he hadn't tried.

Every day when Harry came home for lunch, she greeted him as if he'd been gone for days, truly happy to see him. They were rural enough, she was beginning to feel lonely and isolated. She'd never believed it would be possible, but even living alone in Beckham, if she wanted to be around people, it was easy enough to go outside.

Sundays were her favorite day because they went to church, and she was able to be around other women. On her fifth Sunday at church, she met a lady, who had to be within a year or two of her age.

"I'm Keri White," she said. "I moved here about a month ago as a mail-order bride."

The other woman smiled. "Oh, that must have been a grand adventure. You'll have to tell me all about it!"

"I'd love to! Would you like to come to my house for tea one day this week?"

The other woman, who had introduced herself as Anne Borchard nodded. "I would adore that. My husband and I moved here just a few weeks ago, and I feel like I never have a chance to be around other ladies."

"Why don't you and your husband come and share Sunday dinner with my husband and me, so then you know the way when you come for tea?" Keri absolutely adored the idea of having a friend and even better, being friends with a couple so she and Harry could each spend time enjoying their company.

Anne smiled, nodding. "I was going to serve sandwiches. I'm sure whatever you have will be better."

Keri laughed. "I have a pot roast with vegetables in the oven. I just need to make gravy, and it's ready to eat. I got up early and baked bread, so that's fresh as well."

"Wonderful!" Anne said. "I did make a pie I was planning to serve for supper. I'll go home and get it and then we'll be ready. Let me tell Joseph my plans."

She hurried off and talked to a man, who nodded, and Keri watched her leave the church. She hadn't talked to Anne about what she and Joseph were doing there, so she didn't know if the other woman lived in the country as she did, or if she was there in town.

Harry found her a minute later. "There's a new couple in town I invited for Sunday dinner," Keri said. "I didn't think to ask, but Anne is near my age, and it would be so nice to have a friend around."

Harry nodded. "I was talking to her husband, Joseph. He's opening up a butcher shop here in town. It will be nice to be able to get fresh meat without killing off our own when we want it."

"Oh, I had no idea!" Keri said. "Yes, it will be very nice."

Anne came back in with the pie a moment later. She joined Harry and Keri, and her husband Joseph walked over quickly. "I brought the wagon to church this morning, even though it's a short walk. With Anne in the family way, I try not to make her walk too much."

Keri looked at Anne. "Is there something wrong with the baby?"

Anne shook her head. "Other than having a worried father, there's nothing at all wrong. I saw the doctor this week, and all is going well."

"Then I won't join him in worrying," Keri said with a smile. "Our ranch is a little way out of town."

Anne shrugged. "That doesn't bother me. I'm so excited to have found a friend so quickly here."

Keri nodded. "I've been hoping to find one since I arrived about five or six weeks ago." She thought about what the house was like when they left, but the dishes were done up and the floor was freshly scrubbed. She'd have washed the windows if she knew someone was coming for dinner, but she wasn't terribly worried about them as she'd washed them just a few days before. Her home was immaculate as always.

They went to their wagons, and the other couple followed them out to the ranch. Keri was excited to be hosting her first dinner with friends since she'd married Harry, and she couldn't wait to get everything set on the table just so.

When her belongings had arrived from Massachusetts, the beautiful dishes she'd bought when she'd first sold her book had been with them, and this would be her first chance to use them since she'd arrived.

She hurried into the house ahead of the other couple and got the dishes down from the highest cabinet, having to stand on the very tips of her toes to be able to do so. She put a butter ball on a plate for the bread and set the table quickly.

When Anne came inside, she insisted on helping, so Keri had her put the meat on a platter and surround it with the vegetables that had been cooked with it while she quickly made the gravy.

Keri served everyone a glass of water to go with their meals, and they all ate happily. Harry peppered Joseph with questions about the butcher shop. "Where will you get your meat?" he asked.

"I've made arrangements with a chicken farmer, and a hog farmer. I could still use a rancher to work with me on beef."

As the two men negotiated prices and discussed whether or not Harry's beef would be suitable for the butcher shop, the two women talked about babies. "I want a least a dozen," Anne confessed.

"Not me," Keri said. "I came from a large family. My mother is expecting twins and there are already fourteen of us." She shook her head. "Of course, my first book sold well because it was a humorous look at being the oldest of a large family of children."

"Book? You're a writer?"

Keri nodded. "I sold one book when I was eighteen and haven't sold one since. I do think the mail-order bride adventure book I'm writing will sell though. I'm putting my heroine through absolute misery."

Anne laughed. "If you have any copies of the book you did sell, I'd be happy to buy one from you...but only if you'll autograph it for me."

Keri nodded excitedly. "I've never had the opportunity to autograph something. I like the idea. I brought four or five copies with me from Massachusetts." Six. She'd brought precisely six, but she didn't want to admit to that. It would show that she was prideful about her work if she admitted to knowing exactly how many books she had. Wouldn't it?

After lunch, Anne helped Keri with the dishes, and then Keri went to fetch a copy of her book for Anne. She carefully wrote an inscription, thanking Anne for being her friend, and signed it with a flourish.

As Keri handed Anne the book, she said, "I hope it doesn't scare you off from having multiple children. I'm sure my experiences with my younger siblings aren't indicative of all large families."

Anne smiled, hugging the book to her. "I've never had an autographed book before."

"I've had many," Keri said, "but each one is a treasure to me."

The two women went for a short, healthful walk while the men continued their discussion on beef. "I don't know that they'll ever come to an agreement over those poor cows," Anne said, shaking her head.

"Where are you from?" Keri asked.

"A small town in Upstate New York. There are already two butcher shops in the town we grew up in, and we wanted to move to a place where there wasn't as much competition. Joseph has all of the counters and cases needed to display the meats, so we just need to set up shop, once he has the details worked out for beef products."

"Both men seem to be very involved in their discussion. I do hope they can come to some sort of understanding, even if the understanding is that they shouldn't work together," Keri said with a smile.

"Oh, I do hope they're able to be friends. It would mean we could spend more time together. I'll be making pies for the shop, which is good and bad. I do make good pies, but I don't want that much of my time taken up once the baby comes along."

"When are you due?" Keri asked. Her friend looked perfectly slender to her.

"In about seven months. It's brand new. We've wanted a baby since we married three years ago, but God hasn't blessed us until now."

"I do want children, but I don't want nearly as many as my mother had. Or should I say she's still having? My siblings are an undisciplined lot. Ma did her best with me, and then expected me to raise the rest.

And I helped, but it's hard to put a sister in charge of younger children. At least it was in my family."

As they walked, Keri pointed out different things she was excited about. "That grove of trees is all apple. I can't wait til they bear fruit, and I will be able to do so much with the apples!"

"I hope you're planning on sharing the bounty with your best friend in all Wyoming!"

Keri laughed. "Anne, you *are* my best friend in all Wyoming!"

Their walk was slow and easy, but it felt good to Keri to have a reason to be out for it. Sure, she'd done many chores outside, but it was different sharing the beautiful early summer weather with a friend.

"Tell me about the book you're writing now," Anne suggested.

"Oh, that's not something you should ever ask a writer. They start talking about a book, and they just can't ever stop."

Anne laughed. "I'm sure I'll just ask you questions as we go. I'm really interested!"

"I'm writing a book about a mail-order bride who starts out from Massachusetts like I did, and who goes to South Dakota. She ends up on a train that gets robbed, and then a stagecoach that is rerouted due to floods. I'm on chapter five, and she hasn't even met her poor hero, who only knows her train was robbed and nothing else. He's a sheriff, and once she gets there, he's going to go after her mother's pearls that were stolen while she was on the train, but neither of them knows that's what's going to happen yet."

"That sounds like so much fun! What's your heroine like?"

"Well, she's the oldest of a plethora of children, and she just wants to be away from kids. Unfortunately, there's going to be a fire in the schoolhouse, and the teacher will be injured, and she'll be the best person to fill in for the teacher."

Anne giggled. "Is your method of writing thinking about the worst thing that could possibly happen to your heroine and then writing it that way?"

"Exactly!" Keri said. "It makes books so much more fun; don't you think? Honestly, with this being my first work of fiction, I'm not sure if I'd continue to write things this way, but for this book, it's a great deal of fun."

"I want to be the first to read it! Before you even send it to an editor!"

"I would love that. And you could let me know if the book is worth reading."

"I'm sure it will be. You should delay the couple's wedding night. Like he's planning on having relations one night, and he's called away by a robbery. Then she eats something that doesn't agree with her the next night. And then the next..."

"The next there's a storm, and hail breaks the window in their bedroom."

"Yes! And then next, there's a blizzard in the middle of August, and he has to go and find a group of children who are at the lake and can't find their way home."

"In the middle of the night?" Keri asked.

Anne shrugged. "Works for me if it works for you!"

"I would feel terrible about tormenting my poor couple that way! So, we probably need ten nights' worth of interruptions."

They giggled as they walked, planning several catastrophes for the couple in question. "A wild skunk gets trapped in their house," Anne said.

"A child is left on their doorstep!" Keri suggested. "I'm going to have to make a note of all these when I get back to the house."

"Are you really going to use them?" Anne asked.

"I certainly will! This is the most fun I've ever had plotting out a book. I should hire you as my idea woman. Of course, I'd have to be making money from my writing to do that."

When they got back to the house, both ladies walked inside laughing. The men, who were still in negotiations, both glanced toward the door with smiles on their faces. Harry thought about how good it was to hear Keri laugh. She'd been slowly getting lonelier and lonelier.

All at once, he knew that this couple needed to stay in their lives, and he stuck out his hand to agree to the offer Joseph had just made. The price of beef didn't matter nearly as much as his wife's laughter. Besides, he was already rich anyway.

Chapter Five

On Wednesday, Keri and Anne had tea together, and Keri showed Anne a bit of the book she was working on. Anne read the first two pages, giggling the whole time. "You seriously need to get this published. How far into it are you now?"

"Oh, they just met, and the sheriff is off to find the scoundrels who robbed the train and get her grandmother's pearls back, which means she's there alone with his four children, who won't listen to a word she says."

Anne laughed. "That's amazing. Will they fall in love by the end?"

Keri nodded. "I think so. I mean, I'm not totally sure how it will end because my characters haven't told me yet, but I think they will."

"Oh, did I tell you I read your book? It was wonderful. Funny and informative about the kind of life you led. I couldn't put it down! Joseph finally took it away from me before bed on Sunday, and I finished it before I even did the breakfast dishes on Monday."

"I'm so glad you liked it!"

"The man you talked about as the perfect specimen of manhood and your future husband. That wasn't Harry, was it? I mean, I know you changed the name."

Keri shook her head. "No, not Harry. My brother-in-law, Stanley. My sister married him."

"Oh, that's awful!"

"Not really. After I got to know him a little better, I was glad we didn't marry. He drinks heavily and doesn't treat my sister very well."

"Which sister?" Anne asked.

"I called her Sarah in the book. She's the sister that's a year younger than me."

"Isn't it odd how someone who seemed perfect to us as children turned out to be rotten to the core?"

"Definitely," Keri said. "I know dozens of stories like that. I think my sister regrets that she 'stole' him from me. She's now going to repeat our mother's life, and I'm off across the country, living with a good man and writing my books. I suppose we all know who is making something of her life."

Anne nodded. "I'm sure it hurt at the time, though."

"I can't think of anything that's hurt me more." Keri took a bite of one of the cookies she'd made for their tea. "It was hard to go to the wedding and act like I was happy for her."

"I'm sure it was." Anne shook her head. "I had a crush on Joseph all through school, and for a bit, he courted one of my friends, but she married someone else. He says he would have broken off the courtship for me if she hadn't done it first."

Keri smiled. "I'm glad you married the man you loved."

"What about you?" Anne asked. "Are you in love with Harry?"

Keri bit her lip. "I'm certainly in lust with him. I'm not sure about love yet. Remember, we just met a month ago."

"I guess that makes sense."

Keri got up then and put the pork chops she'd already prepared into the oven for her supper that night. "I do think I'm falling in love with him if that makes sense."

Anne nodded, smiling. "Of course it does. And I think your Edwina, your heroine, will fall in love with the sheriff as well."

"I sure hope so! When he returns with her pearls, I'll start the wedding night fiasco. I'm excited to write all those ideas we came up with."

Anne laughed. "I am looking forward to reading all of that." She looked around the house. "Is your house always this immaculate?"

Keri nodded. "Harry never makes a mess. He's as neat as I am. So the only real thing I have to do all day is cook, sew, do dishes. I'm thankful the garden gives me a respite from utter boredom."

"You should spend more time writing if you really have that much time on your hands. I mean, I know of at least one person who is waiting for that book you're writing and excited to get her hands on it."

"I suppose you're right! I'm just glad I've had a friend to talk to this week. I was getting very lonely."

"I was too," Anne admitted. "Everyone here has been so nice, but I hadn't really connected with anyone the way you and I have. I suppose I could call you a kindred spirit."

"I like that a lot. And I'm thrilled you're here. And that the men worked out a deal they're both happy with. Now we're going to see even more of each other."

"I want you and Harry to eat with us on Sunday for dinner, and then maybe you can come to town for tea on Wednesday. I think no matter who hosts, we should have tea every single Wednesday."

"I agree!" Keri said, smiling. "And we should invite whatever women are new to the area every week. They all get a chance to be our friends, but only one chance."

Anne laughed. "We'll be the most exclusive twosome in all of Wyoming."

After Anne left for the day, Keri peeled potatoes and put them on to boil. The bread for the day was already done. Once the small mess she made cooking was cleaned up, Keri sat down at the table, deciding to follow her friend's advice. She could write when she wasn't working. It wouldn't hurt anyone.

When Harry got home at the end of the day, she had just gotten up to finish supper. "I'm sorry. I got lost in writing after Anne left, and supper will be a little late."

"Did you and Anne enjoy yourselves?"

Keri smiled, nodding. "We really did. We're going to their house for Sunday dinner this week. I hope that's all right with you."

"Absolutely," he said. Truthfully, he'd be happier spending the time alone with her, but he was so happy that she had a friend to keep her from feeling so isolated.

"I should have supper done within ten minutes," she said, hurrying to set the table.

"I'm not upset that it's not ready, you know."

"I appreciate that." She remembered times when her father would come home from working in the fields and supper wasn't on the table. Her father would yell for hours that food wasn't ready when he was. Then he'd drink the night away, and she would want to crawl into a hole somewhere. When her parents were fighting, nothing else could happen in the house. Often, she'd sneaked away into the barn, writing in the hay mow.

She finished readying the food, and sat down at the table with him, her hand immediately going into his for their prayer.

As they ate, he told her about his day, as he usually did. "My foreman, Kevin, likes the idea of marrying so much, he's thinking about sending off for a mail-order bride as well."

"He should! There's no reason for a man to remain single if he doesn't want to. Modern times are bringing wonderful new ways for people to marry."

He smiled and nodded. "That's basically what I told him." He forked up another bite of his meat. "How's your book coming?"

She smiled. "My sheriff just returned from getting his wife's pearl necklace back from the train robbers. Now they are trying to have a wedding night, but with four children in the house, and so many demands on his time, they are not getting very far."

"You're writing about the wedding night?" Harry asked, looking shocked.

"Well, I'm writing about them kissing, and then being interrupted. I won't write about the actual marriage act or anything."

"I don't think you should even write about them kissing. What kind of a reflection would that be on me?"

She frowned. "None at all. I'll continue to use my pen name for the books. No one will ever know your wife wrote them."

"I don't think I like that idea. I would prefer you not write about the wedding night at all." Harry considered the subject closed as soon as he said it. Wives obeyed their husbands.

"I'll take your feelings into consideration," she said, knowing she wasn't going to change what she was doing. She had no idea why he was being such a prude about her writing a few kissing scenes anyway.

He smiled, covering her hand with his. "Thank you."

After the dishes were done, she sat at the table and continued her writing while he did some whittling. He watched her some until he almost sliced into his thumb and decided he should pay more attention to what he was doing when he held a sharp object in his hand. He just wished the evening wouldn't be so silent. Didn't she know they didn't really need the money she would earn from her books?

As soon as it was dark, he stood up. "I think we should go to bed," he said, grinning at her. Bedtime had become his favorite time of day because it meant making love with his wife.

"You go ahead. I'll be in shortly."

He abruptly sat back down. "It's no fun going to bed without you."

She smiled at him. "Let me just finish this paragraph then."

After they'd made love, he immediately fell asleep, but her mind was still churning as she thought about what to throw at her couple next. So she crept out of bed and went back to the table, picking up her pen and starting from where she'd left off.

When Harry woke later, he reached out to pull Keri to him, but she wasn't there. He saw the light from under the closed door of their bedroom and followed it out into the dining room, where she was sitting scribbling away at her book. "You're not sleeping?" he asked.

Keri looked up at him. "I guess I lost track of time. My book is just flowing so well, I hate to leave it."

He frowned. Was her book more important to her than he was? "You need to sleep so you can get up early and cook," he said.

She sighed, finishing the sentence she was working on and standing up. She turned down the lantern and followed him into bed. When he wrapped his whole body around her, she knew there was no waiting until he fell asleep before getting up to write more. No, he was effectively holding her captive.

She'd just have to write more the next day. With a yawn, she fell asleep held close to him.

The next day, she didn't write as soon as she finished the breakfast dishes as she usually did. Instead, she finished the dishes, weeded the garden, watered the garden, did the daily baking, and started lunch. While lunch cooked, she wrote as much as she could, and then again once the lunch dishes were done. She started supper and again sat to write.

By the end of the day, she'd written a full six hours, which was not something she'd been able to do since moving there. It was all about spending her time wisely, and she would be finished soon enough. Writing just made her feel so elated as she sat, writing out everything she thought of.

Harry wasn't quite as kind when supper wasn't on the table as soon as he walked in that night. "Writing again?" he asked.

"Yes, I'm sorry. It'll be ready in five minutes."

He frowned. "You know that we don't need the income from you writing, don't you?" he asked.

She nodded. "I know, but it makes me feel like I'm doing something with my life."

"And being my wife isn't enough?"

She wasn't sure how to answer that. "Yes, of course, it's enough. But this is something I've done since I was a small child. I enjoy it so much. You don't want me to quit, do you?"

"No. You don't need to quit." He did want her to though. She should feel fulfilled just by doing for him, shouldn't she? His mother certainly had.

"Good. I think I'd feel like my soul was ripped in two if I had to quit my writing."

That evening she wrote madly as well. Up until he said it was time for bed anyway. "I don't like it when you get out of bed in the middle of the night to write. I think we should sleep together."

Keri was careful to keep her face even as she nodded. "I won't do it again."

After making love that night, while he held her close and slept, her brain wouldn't stop working on her story. Every paragraph she'd written that day wove its way through her mind, preventing her from sleeping. Oh, how she wished she hadn't told him she wouldn't get up and write anymore, because it was all she could think about. How was she supposed to sleep with words playing their fun little games in her head?

It was the wee hours of the morning before she finally fell asleep, and she had to be up at four. Oh, it was going to be a difficult day, but she would write all she could. After seeing to her chores of course.

When Harry kissed her before leaving for the day, he smiled. "Thanks for not getting up during the night."

She smiled at him sweetly, wishing there was a way to explain how writing made her feel. But to one who didn't write, the feelings would be truly alien. Why, sitting and reading words straight from the dictionary was better than lying in bed wishing she could sleep.

She raced through her chores as soon as he was gone, finding the two or three weeds that had grown overnight, and watering the garden, wishing she didn't live in such an arid place. They had rarely had to water the crops in Massachusetts.

As soon as she was finished, she sat and wrote as many words as she could possibly squeeze out before she had to get ready for lunch. And that's when it hit her. She could set an alarm to give her enough time to make meals before he got home, and write until the alarm went off. Then he would feel as if he got all her time and attention, without ever knowing that she was stopping just to make him feel that way.

It was the perfect solution for her and for him. She could do all she wanted to do for her book, while doing all he wanted her to do for him. Life would be much calmer, and he would be much happier with her.

Though why supper had to be on the table at exactly five in the evening, she would never know. Hopefully, the alarm clock would appease him. If not, she'd have to find some other way.

Chapter Six

Sunday dinner with Anne and Joseph was fun, and they played cards after the dishes were done. Anne wasn't a great cook, but Keri knew that would come with practice and time. Not every girl began cooking for her entire family when she was only eight years old.

At first, they teamed up as couples with Harry and Keri playing against Anne and Joseph, and then the women played the men, which Keri found more fun. She and Anne weren't against distracting the men to win, and they played to win for certain.

After they'd spent most of the day with the other couple, Harry announced it was time for them to go home. Keri was both sad and happy. It had been nice to spend time with the other couple, but as Sunday was her only day off from writing, it was also good to spend some time alone with Harry.

While Harry milked the cows, Keri threw together a quick meal of sandwiches for them to have for supper. Afterward, she wanted to go for a walk, something she and Harry hadn't been doing much of since she'd increased the number of hours per day she was working.

So after the dishes were done, the couple set out for a walk on some of the dirt paths through the ranch, where the men rode their horses. As they walked, Harry pointed straight ahead. "We own the land for as far as the eye can see. I always felt so boxed in back east because we didn't have a lot of land. We were wealthy, but living in the city, limited the amount of land we could hold."

"Do you ever miss your home?"

He shook his head. "Never. I find that Wyoming and being a rancher suit me so much better than being a banker ever did."

"Wait, I didn't realize you were a banker for a while."

"Almost a year when my father died, and I decided to leave. I miss Mother at times, but truly not very often. She was very rigid in her beliefs of how things should be, and I prefer to be a little more relaxed. For instance, she would shudder if she saw what I wear to church every Sunday. Back east I was always in a suit and tie. Here, I can wear a suit, but I usually just wear one of my plaid shirts and a pair of Levis."

She smiled. "I like how your bottom looks in a pair of Levis."

He was shocked for a moment, and then started to laugh, putting his arm around her shoulders and pulling her closer. "You do keep me on my toes, Keri."

"I do my best." She opened her mouth to tell him about some of the failed wedding nights she was writing and then thought better of it. She knew he didn't approve of her writing something so risqué. "I love the countryside here. Are there any wild berries I should be watching for?"

"All the usual. Raspberries, and cherries, and chokecherries, and blackberries. Even some huckleberries in late July, but you have to really hunt for those."

"Any that you prefer to the others?" she asked. It would be fun to spend a day with a basket and see what berries she could find.

"I like blackberries and raspberries best. Well, no, I like apples best, but they're not berries."

She laughed. "With all the apple trees we have, I'll be able to make your apple tooth sing."

"My apple tooth?"

She shrugged. "I have a sweet tooth. You should be able to have an apple tooth."

He shook his head. "I've heard Shakespeare made up all kinds of words. Do all writers think it's all right to do that?"

"I don't know about others because I don't know any writers, but I certainly think it's all right. I love making up new words."

"You may need to include a glossary in all your books with the words you've made up appearing there."

"That's not a bad idea at all."

They reached a shallow stream, and he jumped over it and offered a hand as she walked across on rocks. "I'm glad I don't have to haul water from here to water our garden," she said, shaking her head. "That pump in the kitchen makes me feel like I live in the future."

He chuckled. "I'm glad you enjoy it!"

"Oh, trust me, I do." They'd walked less than a minute past the stream when she spotted some berries. "Blackberries! You don't mind if I pick them, do you?"

He shook his head. "Where will you put them though?"

"I mean I'll come back tomorrow and pick them," she said, shaking her head, thinking it would cut into her writing time, but berries were only ripe for a short while, and her book could be worked on mentally while she picked the berries.

"I think that's a much better idea than picking them now. I'd offer my hat, but I don't need to have berry stains all over my head."

She giggled at the idea. "I like that thought. May I borrow your hat?" she asked.

"No."

"You're a spoil sport!"

They turned around there and walked back toward the house. "I think we'll be back a little after dark as it is," he said, shaking his head. "It's not good to get caught out here after dark with no gun, and I didn't bring one."

"We'll hurry," she told him.

When they got back to the house, she looked around, realizing everything was in its place just as it should be. "I'm glad you're as tidy as I am," she said. "I like that I don't have to spend all my time picking up after you." Her father had often tracked mud into the house, and she would have to clean up after him. Her ma had done little work around the house as soon as Keri was old enough to do her share and then some.

"Was your father messy?"

She laughed. "He stomped through mud and right into the house all the time. Of course, Ma never complained because it was always me cleaning it not her."

"I don't think I would have liked your childhood."

"What childhood?" She knew it was rude to say, but it was true. She'd been expected to raise her younger siblings from a very young age. Life had always been hard because all Ma wanted to do was have more babies.

She went to their room to dress for bed, but as she started to pull her nightgown over her head, Harry took it from her, placing it atop the dresser, and instead his hands came around her cupping her breasts.

When she turned in his arms and eagerly unbuttoned his shirt, she was glad she'd taken the day off from writing to spend with him. He truly made her feel as if she was cherished, and she couldn't ask for more from life than that.

She was busy all week picking blackberries, canning jams and pie filling, and having tea with Anne. By Friday, she was ready to sit down and do nothing but write, and thankfully, she'd earned the right to do so. The house was immaculate, stew was cooking on the stove top for supper, and her fingers were itching to get back to work.

She read over a bit of what she'd written so far, and couldn't help but giggle as she did so. The words sounded so unfamiliar to her as if someone else had written them, and the laughter was a full belly laugh because she didn't have any idea what she'd said when she'd written it.

For Keri, sometimes as she wrote, it felt like something magical happened and words just came out of her, though she had no idea where they came from. She would love the words when she read back over them, but it was hard to believe they'd come from deep within her.

She set the alarm before she put pen to paper, knowing that she would forget to set the table before Harry came home otherwise. It was hard to be a housewife and a writer because writing took over her entire body, mind, and soul.

When the alarm went off, she didn't want to stop, but she turned the alarm off, set it for four, and returned it to the bedroom so they would wake up on time to milk the cows in the morning. She knew he would have a problem with her setting an alarm to remember to be a wife.

Supper was on the table as he walked in the door, and she could see by his smile that Harry felt everything was as it should be simply because she'd had supper ready at his designated time. It didn't matter what else she had to do with her time, if supper was on the table at five, it was a good day.

He told her about two calves moving away from the herd and how he and his men had searched for them over supper. "Cows almost never have twins, and this one heifer did. Those twins get into more mischief than the rest of the herd combined! We're always off chasing them somewhere or getting them untangled from weeds. I don't know how they manage it, but they do."

Keri smiled. "They sound like fun. We had two sets of twins in my family, and they were more mischievous than the rest. Twins seem to be able to communicate without words, or with their own language as my ten-year-old twin sisters have. One can make strange grunting sounds, and they both jump up and do something at the same time. It's so strange."

"Didn't you say your mom was having twins again?" he asked.

She nodded. "It's her third set of twins, and she's so happy about it. How can anyone be quite that happy about so many children?"

"I do want at least a few children," he said.

"That's a reasonable number. I just hope I'm not like my mother who has twins often. One at a time seems to be the best way to do things."

"I agree. It's best for calves as well. No one should have to carry two babies at once."

"Well, kittens seem to be different. Cats can carry several."

"So can dogs," he said. "Would you like a puppy for the house?"

"I'd prefer a kitten who could chase away any mice that decide to take up residence."

"Really?" He shrugged. "I've never had a cat."

"We had a couple of barn cats growing up. Dogs make me nervous."

"I'll see if anyone in town has a litter. A kitten would be fine with me if you don't mind one. And you know how to care for one because I really don't."

"I do," she said, smiling. "I love the idea of having a kitten. It's been so long, and they're so much fun to play with."

"All right. I'm sure someone in church will have a kitten or two they want to get rid of."

"Probably. I think the world needs more cats, but I have a feeling most people wouldn't agree with that statement."

After supper dishes were done, she sat down to write. "Do you mind if I write this evening?" she asked. Keri was becoming aware of the fact that he didn't really like it when she spent her time writing. At least she had time during the day when she could do as she pleased. Oh, she should probably be making a quilt or something, but writing kept her hands and her mind busy, and that kept her happy.

He nodded. "I'll whittle then."

"What are you making?" she asked.

"It's going to be a critter, but I haven't decided which kind yet."

She frowned. "Have you ever actually whittled anything before?"

He laughed, shaking his head. "I always get to the point where I think it should take shape, and I end up throwing it out because of how ugly it is."

Keri laughed at that. "You just keep practicing then."

"I think I will."

As Keri wrote, the sounds of his knife against the wood sounded so right and so natural. It was the perfect sound to write to.

As soon as it was dark, Harry set down his knife and put the misshapen block of wood beside it. "It'll be something."

"Maybe you should make eggs to start with. Then we can paint them pretty colors and call them Easter eggs."

"Buy a book, get an Easter egg!"

She laughed. "That might just work."

As she set her pen down beside the paper she'd been writing on, she knew that her book was close to being finished. Another chapter or two, and it would be done. What a joy it would be to share her finished book with a publisher. Of course, first, Anne had to read it and let her know if it was good enough.

Her mind was still on her book as they went to their bedroom to undress for sleep. This time she didn't even bother getting out her nightgown, instead just walking into his arms as soon as her clothes were off. "Have I told you yet that I consider myself very fortunate that you were the man waiting for the train and for me when I got to Wyoming?" she asked.

"You haven't, but I think I understand. My first look at you had me worried I'd married a very sickly woman, but now, I'm so glad it was you." He kissed her then, and they didn't talk for a while.

Her mind still buzzed with ideas for her ending of her book as he fell asleep. She would have to remember how to fall asleep soon, or she would be a mess again, but it was good to care so passionately about a book she was writing. That hadn't happened since her first book, and she thought it showed. She was sure it did.

Keri knew she had a book that was worth reading, for the first time in a long while. She didn't know if it was because she was writing it from a better place, both physically and mentally, or because it was just that much better than what she'd been writing for the past few years. Either way, she was happy that it felt right for the first time in a very long while.

Soon she'd be able to send it to her agent, and she knew she'd get a better response this time. This book was as funny as her first, and even though this was her first work of fiction, she knew it would sell. It felt too good not to sell.

She only wished she didn't have to use a pen name for it, but Harry would not be happy if his name was tied to her book.

Chapter Seven

On Sunday, Keri packed a picnic lunch, and they drove out to Willow Lake to eat their lunch on the banks. There were others there as well. There were couples picnicking and families boating and playing in the water. It felt like a glorious lazy day for Keri who had spent the last two days writing every minute she found herself without something more important to do.

As they ate the chicken she'd fried, she looked around her, enjoying watching the others there and thinking a scene at a lake needed to be part of the book she was writing. Maybe while the children played in the lake, her hero and heroine could finally admit they loved one another. Or maybe not. She wasn't sure, but a lake scene was absolutely necessary.

"I thought the sermon was really good today," Harry said.

Keri nodded. "What was your favorite part?" She wouldn't admit it aloud, but she'd daydreamed through most of the service and had no idea what the sermon had been about.

"Loving your neighbor," he said. "There's an old widower that lives only a five-minute walk up the road from us. Perhaps we could invite him to supper one evening? Or you could take him a meal so he didn't have to cook for himself?"

"I'd love that. I feel like the only people I know here other than you are Anne and Joseph. I need to learn to be more a part of the community."

He nodded. "Why don't we stop by on the way home and see if he wants to have supper with us tomorrow? Would that work for you?"

She smiled and nodded. "Do you always take sermons to heart?"

"I try. Sometimes it's harder than others."

As they drove home, he stopped in front of a farmhouse, not too far from their own home on the ranch. He jumped down from the wagon and hurried up to the door. "Mr. Walters? I wanted to invite you to supper with us tomorrow night?"

"I'd like that. My daughter makes sure I'm fed on Sundays, but I'm on my own the rest of the week."

"Let us start helping with that. You can come to supper any night you want."

Mr. Walters smiled widely. "I would adore that. You must have listened to the sermon today."

"I always listen to the sermon," Harry said, raising his hand in a wave. He turned to go back to the wagon but stopped. "Supper is at five."

"I'll be there."

As he drove the rest of the way home, Harry was feeling pleased with himself for finding someone who could use their help. Keri was such a good cook, and she was always fixing meals anyway. It didn't hurt for her to fix enough for one more person. "I invited him to come to supper whenever he wanted," Harry told her. "Just always fix enough for three. If he doesn't come, the chickens will be happy with the extra food."

"All right. I can do that." She was already cooking enough for supper for their lunch the following day. Adding a little extra—even some for Mr. Walters to take home with him for lunch would be easy enough. She wished there was someone taking care of the older man.

The following night, she made a roast with potatoes, carrots, and fresh bread. She was certain the older man would be pleased to have the homecooked meal. When he arrived shortly before five, she was just putting supper on the table. Her book, which she'd worked on much of the afternoon was in a neat stack on a shelf, and out of the way.

She opened the door to him, smiling. "Mr. Walters, welcome! I'm just finishing putting supper on the table, and Harry should be here any moment."

Mr. Walters nodded, smiling a big grin with only a few teeth visible. "Thank you for the invitation," he said, wandering around for a moment.

"What would you like to drink with supper? Coffee, tea, or milk?"

"Milk please," he said, reaching for the pages of her book. She started to stop him, but decided it wouldn't hurt for him to read a page before putting it down. She didn't think her book would appeal to men at all. "What is this?"

"Just a book I'm writing," she said softly. "Do you enjoy reading?" She mixed up the gravy while she talked to him.

"I do. A great deal."

She saw him take the pages and sit down at the table. It wasn't long before he was laughing. "You have a knack for storytelling."

"Thank you. I have one book published, and I hope this one will be soon."

"It's wonderful. I love how you keep interrupting that poor couple's wedding night."

She grinned. "My friend and I came up with that together. Do you know the new butcher in town?"

"Oh, I've met him, but haven't really gotten to know him yet."

"His wife and I have become friends, and it was her idea for me to do that. It was my idea for all of the disasters on her way to meet him."

Mr. Walters chuckled. "A book is only fun if there are multiple disasters."

She laughed. "I keep looking at what's happening with them and wondering what's the worst thing that could happen. Then I write that."

"This will be the best book. I just know it. You need to promise me an autographed copy as soon as it's in print. I'll pay for it, but you have to inscribe it."

"I promise!"

The door opened and Harry came in. As always, he immediately hung his hat on a peg near the door before going into the kitchen and washing his hands. "It's good to see you, Mr. Walters."

"You have a very talented wife," Mr. Walters told him. "This book of hers is quite funny."

Harry glanced at Keri, smiling. "I think she's pretty special. I've just about decided to keep her."

"You definitely need to keep her," Mr. Walters said. "She promised me an autographed book, and I need you to help me hold her to that."

"I sure will," Harry said, moving to the table to sit with Mr. Walters, who carefully took the pages back to the shelf where he'd found them.

"I saw a few more of your calves on my land today," Mr. Walters said.

"I'm sorry about that," Harry replied. "I think we've got them all rounded up. I'm sure glad you're not still working your land because those calves would be ruining your crops."

Mr. Walters chuckled. "Now it's not a problem. I should sell you my land anyway, and just keep the house."

"If you decide you want to do that, I'm open to it." Harry had already bought up all the land surrounding Mr. Walter's land. He would happily take more, as he wanted the ranch he was building to create an empire for him and his descendants. He had dreams, and he wanted them all to come to reality.

As they ate, they talked about the area and Mr. Walters decided on the spot he wanted to sell his land. "None of my kids or grandkids want to farm or ranch. And with you owning all the land surrounding mine, it just makes sense to sell to you."

"I agree," Harry said. He especially wanted the small lake that was on Mr. Walter's property. It would make it easy for him to cut a path of water through his land and not have to haul it from so far for his cattle. "We can talk about it after supper, or whenever you're ready. I don't want you to feel like I invited you to supper to get my hands on your land though because that couldn't be further from the truth."

While the men talked, Keri thought about her book some more. Her heroine didn't like that the sheriff was always out doing things that put him in danger. Perhaps she could have him buy a spread of land and start a ranch there. She'd have to ask Harry some pertinent questions, but she was certain she could make that work with her story.

And now she had an ending to write toward. Why, she was sure her book could be finished in a few days if she worked hard on it. She wanted to get up and dance, but she had a feeling the men would think she'd lost her mind.

At that moment, all she wanted to do was sit down with her pages and finish the book, but she knew better. First, she had to do the dishes and pretend interest in the meal she'd made.

When they'd finished, she brought the pie she'd made that day from the kitchen. "Blackberry pie anyone?" She dearly hoped they'd say no, so she could get started on the dishes, but she knew that wasn't going to happen.

Mr. Walters's face lit up when he heard the word pie. "Blackberry is my favorite of all the pies my wife used to make."

She set the pie on the table and got three small plates, serving a piece to each of them. "Do either of you need more milk before I sit down again?" she asked.

Both men pushed their glasses toward her, and she poured milk into them as well as her own. As she ate her pie, the men talked about the price of the land, and she had no interest. No her mind was with her heroine, Edwina, and how relieved the poor girl would be once she had her sheriff being a full-time rancher instead of a sheriff.

She could even write sequels about the children. Oh, she had ideas, and they were filling her head.

"What do you think, Keri?" Harry asked.

Keri grinned. “My mind was somewhere else. What did you ask me?”

Harry shook his head, laughing. “I was just trying to include you in the conversation. Go back to your thoughts.”

She grinned, feeling a bit sheepish, but that was all right. They knew she was a writer and therefore lived in her own head most of the time anyway.

When she finished her pie, she got up and started on the dishes while the men talked. That way as soon as Mr. Walters headed home, she would be able to start writing again.

To her chagrin, he stayed until it was fully dark, and then Harry walked home with him. Mr. Walters hadn’t brought a gun, and Harry felt as if it should be there for protection if you were out after dark.

While Harry was gone, Keri sat down and wrote out three full pages. It wasn’t nearly as much as she’d wanted to get done that evening, but it was better than nothing. Oh, how she was ready to have this book finished and off to her publisher. She knew this one would sell, and she was ready to make it happen.

When Harry came in, she immediately put her pages aside to go to bed with him. She knew he’d be unhappy if she continued to write while he was sleeping. How she wished he understood that the hours while others slept could be the best writing hours of the day.

She was able to keep herself in bed until after two, but then she crept out of the bedroom to get more words in. Without the alarm, four came without her realizing, and she hurried into the kitchen to cook while Harry stomped outside to milk the cows. She knew he hated waking up without her in bed beside him, but she really needed to get this book out of her head and on paper, so she could think about other things than just the story.

She put her pages onto the shelf where they could be easily ignored while they ate breakfast. When Harry came back inside, she greeted him with a morning kiss. "Do you know if Mr. Walters is coming for supper tonight?"

Harry shook his head. "I don't know, but plan for him." He watched her for a moment. "Why were you up so early?"

Keri frowned. "I can't sleep when I'm this deep into a book. All I can think about is where the story is going. I mean, I'll sleep for an hour or two, but then I'll wake up again, compelled to write. So I do."

"I don't know that you should be writing then. It's not good for you to go without sleep."

"But if I don't write, then the stories stay in my head, and I'm thinking about them all the time anyway. I have to get them out somehow." She put their breakfast on the table, knowing he was upset with her, but unsure how to fix things. She was doing the best she could to put the story out of her mind while he was there.

"It takes over your whole life!"

She nodded. "I'm sorry, but it's always been that way. Even when I write nonfiction, my mind is always playing with what I should include, and what should come next. I wish things were different for you, but it is how I'm used to living."

"But what will happen when the babies come? You'll need your sleep to stay focused on them."

"I honestly don't know. I guess I should have told you I get this way when we first met, so you could decide if you still wanted to marry me."

He sighed, wrapping his arms around her. "Of course, I want to be married to you. It's just going to take some adjustment. On both of our parts, I think."

"So, you're not mad?"

"Mad, no. Concerned, yes. How long do you take off between books?"

She shrugged. "As long as my brain will let me. We'll see what happens after this one. I already have stories playing in my head for the children of the couple."

As they ate breakfast, she tried her best to be in the moment, and enjoying his company. She asked what he would be doing that day, and he talked about the fences the calves had broken the day before.

"Do you think you'll buy Mr. Walters's land?"

He nodded. "I do. We've been talking about it as you know, and adding his land to our property would be a huge help. I believe I'm going to buy his house as well, and then I'll let him live there until he passes. Then I'll have a house where my foreman can live away from the men."

"That's a wonderful idea. None of his children want the house?"

Harry shook his head. "Even the daughter who still lives here is planning to move back east with her family once he passes. They're just not people meant to farm or ranch. They're city people."

"It sounds like selling is in his best interest then."

Chapter Eight

Wednesday was tea day with Anne, so Keri made tea cakes for them to eat. She hoped Anne would want to read more of what she'd written so she herself could continue writing. It was hard to get all the writing she wanted to do done around her other chores and Harry's rigid sleep schedule. She wasn't sure he'd ever understand how her mind worked and why she was so eager to write during the night while he slept.

Anne was in a good mood when she walked into the house, removing her bonnet. "All right, catch me up. Where are you on the book?"

Keri was thrilled her friend wanted to hear about it. "Well, Harry helped me figure out the ending I want, even though he doesn't know it. I think I can be done by the end of next week if I manage my time wisely."

"Really?" Anne asked. "That's so exciting." She looked at the pages in a neat stack on one corner of the table. "Do you mind if I read while we have our tea and treats?"

"Not at all. I was hoping you'd want to because then I can write new words."

"Let's do it then."

Keri poured the tea and put the cakes on the table, and then she sat down and put pen to paper once again. It felt so good to sit and write while Anne giggled over the words she'd written. She had no idea how she'd been a solitary writer for so long when she felt so encouraged by both Anne and Mr. Walters to finish the book.

She scribbled out her words and Anne laughed. It made for the perfect afternoon in Keri's opinion. She had her alarm set for four, so she would know to put the pie she'd made into the oven for their supper. She knew poor Harry had to be getting sick of her pot pies, but he never said a word when he sat down to another. He was a good husband.

Finally, when the alarm went off at four, Anne looked up from the book. "What time is it?"

"Four," Keri said. "I have to put supper in the oven." As she got up to do so, her friend hurriedly tied her bonnet at her chin.

"I'll see you Sunday," Anne called. "I have to get supper in the oven too!" And with that, her friend was gone.

Keri realized as she left that they'd spoken very little to one another during the two hours Anne was there, but she knew they'd both had a marvelous time. Anne had been more than a little entertained by the pages she'd written while she'd been happy as a lark writing new words.

Mr. Walters came for supper that night, and he immediately sat at the table with Keri's story around him. "Do you want something to drink with your pages, Mr. Walters?"

Mr. Walters looked up with a sheepish grin. "Milk would be nice." And then his mind was back in the pages she'd written, and he kept chuckling at her words. It felt good to have two people who were as interested in her book and how it would end as she was.

When Harry came in, she'd just finished putting supper on the table, and she took the pages from Mr. Walters. "Sorry," she told the older man. "You can read more the next time you come over."

Mr. Walters sighed. "I'm going to start coming over for lunch and staying until supper so I can catch up on that book!"

"You're welcome anytime." Keri took her seat at the table.

"This smells delicious," Mr. Walters said. "What did you make for us?"

"It's a beef pot pie. One of my favorites. I love chicken pot pie as well. I made it a lot for my large family as I was growing up. It stretched further than a lot of other things would have."

"How big is your family?" he asked.

"I currently have thirteen younger sisters and brothers, but my ma is pregnant with her third set of twins, so this will be fifteen brothers and sisters."

"Oh, dear. That is a large family. I thought my Alice and I had a big family with eight children, but that's only half of what your parents had."

Keri nodded. "Our family was much too big. It was chaos all the time."

He chuckled. "That's how you know it's a good family, though. When chaos reigns."

"It wouldn't have been so bad if my mother had actually taken responsibility for my siblings. She felt like once I was old enough to help, her job was done, and it was my job to take care of the others."

Mr. Walters nodded. "Many large families are that way. Alice and I made sure that we were the ones who took care of our children though. Well, Alice took care of our children."

"That's how it should be," Keri agreed.

Mr. Walters looked at Harry. "What about you? How many siblings do you have?"

"I'm an only child," Harry responded.

"That's sad," Mr. Walters said. "Do you two want children?"

"I'd like three or four," Keri said. "I would have time to care for them, take care of the house, do the cooking, mending, and still get my writing done. Any more than that, and I would be hard-pressed to keep up."

Harry smiled. "I want an even dozen."

Mr. Walters looked between the two of them. "I'm not sure how the two of you are going to meet in the middle about that, but I think you'll find a way."

"Maybe we'll have to hire a housekeeper to help around here," Harry said with a shrug. "Then Keri could spend her days writing as much as she wants to write. I think she'd be pleased with that anyway."

Keri smiled. "There's no need at the moment. I have more than enough time to take care of everything. If I start having twins like my mother did, it would be nice to have help." She would never enlist her children to take care of one another. She'd quit writing first, and she was sure a piece of her would die.

She almost laughed at how melodramatic she was being in her thoughts, but decided the people with her wouldn't understand at all. It was hard to have a story going in her head and be with humans at the same time.

After the supper dishes were finished, Harry and Mr. Walters went onto the front porch and talked about the sale for a bit. Apparently, they still hadn't agreed on terms, but that was just fine with Keri. It gave her a little more time to write.

To her surprise, before Harry was even inside for the night, she finished her book. She hadn't realized how close she was to wrapping it up until that moment. She started her first read-through on it, planning to fix whatever errors caught her eye as she went, but she wrote a very clean first draft, and there was little to fix.

Perhaps after Anne and Mr. Walters went through it, they would have suggestions.

When Harry came into the house, it was again after dark, and she immediately followed him to the bedroom to his surprise. "I thought I'd find you scribbling away at your book."

"I finished it while you were talking with Mr. Walters. I can't wait to hear what my agent thinks. I already wrote to him and told him what I had coming to him soon, and he seemed excited."

"That's wonderful!" Harry said. "I get my wife back!"

She smiled. "You certainly do." Her arms went around his neck and she kissed him. Finally, they had time to be just a husband and wife, while she waited for a response from her agent.

The entire next day was spent scrubbing the house and weeding the garden. She'd thought she'd have so much to do after finishing her book, but unfortunately, she hadn't gotten behind on anything, so she had as little to do as always.

She walked through the ranch, looking for more berries to pick so she would be able to have some canning projects to work on at least, and she found some berries, but not more than she would use in a single pie.

Deciding she'd make the pie for supper was easy enough, and she added it to the fried chicken and mashed potatoes she was already planning. Hopefully Mr. Walters would come, and he could read the rest of the book before Sunday, when she could pass it off to Anne until they had tea together on Wednesday.

She itched to start on the next book, about one of the sheriff's daughters, but she knew better. If this book didn't sell, there was no point in writing sequels for it. Why would anyone do such a thing?

She'd have to do something else to keep busy. Maybe she could make a new dress for herself. She had the fabric. Keri would stay busy for a short while if she did that.

First, she went through all of Harry's clothes that were in their bedroom, finding a few pairs of Levis that needed to be mended along with a few of his winter shirts. He could use a new hat and scarf for the winter, she noted, so she began a list of things she could make for him to keep her mind busy. It was hard when she only wanted to do one thing, but she had other things she needed to do first.

When Mr. Walters didn't come for supper on Thursday night, she decided she would walk the book over to him on Friday morning, and tell him she was desperate for his feedback.

So, after supper, she and Harry sat on the front porch swing, just enjoying the peacefulness of the country. "Are you happy your book is done?" he asked.

"In some ways. I mean, it's always good to finish one and feel the sense of accomplishment wash over you, but in this case, the next books I'm thinking of writing will be sequels to this one, so there's no point in even starting them if my agent doesn't think he can sell this one." She shook her head. "That leaves me with a good amount of free time on my hands. I'm going to make myself a new dress with some of the fabric I have, and I think I'll knit you a new scarf and hat for winter, but there's not enough to do to fill all the free time I'll have." She frowned at him. "Do you think you could trudge mud inside when you come home tomorrow, and then I'll have reason to scrub the floors?"

He gaped at her for a moment before laughing. "You can't sit still, can you? You have to always be doing something."

Keri nodded. "I do. And if I am not utterly exhausted at bedtime, my brain will keep me awake as it plans the next book or even the one after that. I need to absolutely exhaust myself to sleep."

"I've never met anyone quite like you," Harry said, smiling at her. "I would think you'd be happy to have some time to relax a little, but I don't think you know how to relax."

"I don't! I mean, I like to read, but I've read all the books I have, and I'd rather write than read anyway."

He chuckled. "I'll take you into town tomorrow after lunch, and you can get some yarn to make me that scarf and hat. I always wear a stocking cap under my cowboy hat in the winter. I get so cold here."

"I can understand that perfectly," she said. "I can make you some more socks as well. I've noticed that most of your socks are wearing out."

"I'd like that. How long of a break will you take before you start your next book?"

"Until I hear from my agent. It's strange because I'm difficult when I'm writing because it's all I want to do, but then between books, I'm difficult because I'm so desperately trying to find things to fill my time. I need a kitten."

"Being married to you is going to be the greatest and most rewarding challenge of my life. I can already see that." Harry leaned down and kissed her.

"Oo, that's something we can do to keep me busy." She stood and took his hand. "It'll be dark soon anyway."

"Not for a couple of hours."

"I think I can keep you busy that long," she said, pulling him toward the bedroom.

"I think I like not-writing Keri better than writing Keri."

"I like writing Keri better," she said. "Writing Keri makes me feel like I'm leaving my mark on the world."

"You're leaving your mark on me regardless."

She laughed, pulling his head down for a kiss. "I guess I am."

IMMEDIATELY AFTER THE dishes were done the following morning, Keri took her pages to Mr. Walters. "I'm sorry to bother you, but I finished, and I want you to read it before Sunday, so I can give it to my friend Anne to read and then send it to my agent."

Mr. Walters took the pages excitedly. "I'll have it done by supper tonight, and I'll bring it by when I beg to be included in your evening meal."

"You don't need to beg. I always make enough for three, and we enjoy your company."

He nodded. "Thank you. I'll bring it back in a few hours."

As she walked back to the house, she passed a few more blackberry bushes, and she hurried home to get her pail so she could pick the berries. At least it was something that would keep her busy while she waited for feedback from her two readers.

When Harry arrived home for lunch that day, he noticed the berries. "You found more?"

She nodded. "There were a few ripe bushes between here and Mr. Walters's house, so I went back with my pail and made short work of them. I don't know if these will be jam or pie filling, but whichever they end up being, I know they'll be delicious."

She put their lunch on the table, and they ate quickly. She was excited to get to town and find some yarn and maybe some more fabric. She would love to make curtains and a tablecloth that matched for the dining room, and she thought curtains with flowers would look beautiful on the windows in the kitchen. It was fun to have so many options. But her mind was still on her next book.

Chapter Nine

Heading into town that afternoon was fun for Keri. Harry seemed perfectly happy to be there with her, and they talked about everything and nothing along the drive there.

While she went into the store to choose her purchases, Harry stayed outside, talking to a couple of men who were playing a game of checkers in front of the store. They were older men, and Keri was certain they were giving Harry tips on how to be the best rancher he could be.

She found some green yarn that would match his eyes and bought several skeins of it, knowing she wanted to use it for his hat and scarf and maybe even socks. She also got some darker color skeins for more socks. After looking through his drawers and doing his laundry for six weeks, she had yet to find a pair that hadn't been mended at least a couple of times. She had nothing against mended socks, but she thought he needed new ones as well.

She found a pretty pattern for curtains and a matching tablecloth for the dining room, and she also added more fabric for curtains for the kitchen. Wanting to wait until she heard back from her agent just might kill her because she would have to fill her days with other things. Thankfully, it was summer, and she would have gardening to do, but that only took her an hour per day to water everything and take care of any new weeds that sprang up overnight.

She bought thread and even a crate of jars so she would have them available for canning that fall. Not that she hadn't already started canning. It was almost time for her to be able to pick huckleberries as well, and she hoped that she could convince Anne it was a good way to spend an afternoon together.

When she had purchased everything, and the merchant's son was carrying her items to the wagon, she stepped outside to see Harry grinning down into a basket he was holding. "What's that?" she asked, walking over and peering into it. She gasped when she spotted two kittens, a white one sleeping atop a black and white one. "For me?"

He nodded. "They were the last from two different litters. The white one is a tom, and the black and white is a female."

"Are they mine?" Keri couldn't believe she would have two small kittens of her very own.

"Yup. You said you wanted kittens."

"Oh, thank you!" She couldn't help but reach into the basket and pluck the white one from its spot atop the other, snuggling it to her chest. "What's your name?"

Harry chuckled. "All right, put him back in the basket, and we'll head home. Did you find everything you needed?"

She nodded. "Yes, I did." She saw that the wagon had been loaded while she talked to Harry and snuggled the kitten. She reluctantly put the kitten back into the basket and waited as Harry set the basket in the middle of the wagon seat before helping her up.

On the drive home, Keri couldn't quit looking at the kittens, and she couldn't stop smiling. He'd definitely found the right way to distract her from her writing.

Once they were home, she carried the basket with the kittens into the house while leaving him to deal with the rest of her purchases. After settling the kittens, she went to the kitchen to work on supper, while Harry went to join his men for the rest of the afternoon.

They'd gone to Joseph's butcher shop before heading to the mercantile in town, so she had a fresh pork loin to turn into their supper. She cooked it the same way she'd always cooked pork loin, with potatoes, carrots, and a bit of seasoning. The bread for the day was finished and ready, and they'd share that with Mr. Walters who had promised her he was coming for supper.

She was sitting on the floor playing with the kittens when Mr. Walters arrived with her pages in hand. He smiled when he saw the kittens. "Those two are going to get into some mischief."

"Nah," she responded. "They're too sweet for that."

He just laughed. "I finished your book. Re-read what I had already read and read the new pages. It's excellent. It made me laugh out loud more times than I can count."

"And you found the ending satisfying? I was a little worried that I rushed it too much and people wouldn't be happy."

"It was perfect. You don't need to worry about anything."

Keri breathed a sigh of relief. "Did you find all the interruptions to their wedding night too candid? Harry was worried that I would offend people with that."

"Not at all. Really. I loved every word, and I don't even think I'm your primary audience."

She smiled. "I thought all my readers would be women, for certain."

"I just like to read, and I prefer a happily ever after at the end." Mr. Walters gently laid all the pages on the shelf where she kept them. "I think you have a winner here."

"Would you like me to inscribe one of my first books for you? All about being the eldest of fourteen children?"

"Is it as funny as this book was?" he asked.

She nodded. "I think so. And the best part is, it was all true. I never thought I'd be writing fiction, but ideas came to me as I was on my journey here."

"I think you're wonderful with fiction. I can't wait to see what you do with non-fiction."

She stood and hurried from the room, coming back with a copy of her first book, and opening it to carefully autograph it. "To my friend Mr. Walters, I'm so happy to be able to call you both neighbor and friend. Carrie Stockwell."

Stockwell was her mother's maiden name, and she found she enjoyed using it as her pen name. And Carrie was a more common spelling of her own name. She still wondered how her mother had found it within herself to be able to spell her name as creatively as she had.

When she handed Mr. Walters the book, he read her inscription and smiled. "I look forward to reading it. Having an author marry my closest neighbor is one of the highlights of my life! Especially since my Alice died."

"When did you lose her?" Keri asked, not sure if she should show interest or just sympathy, but she found people liked to talk about dead loved ones, so she would try that first.

"Five years ago. Doc thinks it was her heart."

"I'm sorry for your loss. How long were you married?"

His whole face lit up at the question. "I was eighteen and she was fifteen. She was the sweetest girl in our little school, and I asked her to marry me, and her pa said yes. We were married fifty-eight years, and they were the best years of my life. Sometimes, I wonder how I can keep going without her, but then I remember she's waiting for me, and she'll be mine again."

"It must be very strange to live without her after that long," Keri said. "How long did you live here?"

"We moved here when I was thirty-five. It was a long time ago. I kept seeing advertisements about the free land waiting in Oregon Territory. So, I talked to my wife, and we packed up our house and our children, and we went to Independence, Missouri, and we got here about a year later."

Her brows drew together in confusion. "I thought it only took six months to walk the Trail."

He smiled. "It does. What people forget is we had to go all the way to Oregon City, claim our land, and then come back to where we wanted to settle. Usually a year from start to finish, because people would get stuck in Oregon until the snow melted."

"I had no idea. I want you to tell me everything about the journey!" she said. "All I've heard is that the hardship was remarkable."

He smiled. "My wife kept a beautiful journal of what it was like for her on the trail with our four children."

"May I read it?" She was hoping that's why he mentioned it, but he hadn't offered it.

He nodded. "I think it will help you understand what a lot of people around here went through to get the land we wanted."

"I'm excited! That sounds like something I would want to dive right into." When she felt something pulling on her dress, she looked down to see the kittens each climbing her dress. "I think someone wants to see me."

Mr. Walters laughed. "What are you naming them?"

"I'm not sure yet. Any suggestions?" She scooped a kitten up in each hand and snuggled them to her neck.

"You got a tom and a girl there?" he asked.

She nodded. "Yup, one of each. And they're from different litters. I hope they have a million babies, and then the barn will never have another mouse."

He laughed. "I think you should name them Alice and Jackson."

"Why?" she asked. She knew his wife's name was Alice, but she had no idea where Jackson was coming from.

"I never properly introduced myself, did I? I'm Jackson Walters."

She smiled. "I was hoping that would be your answer. Yes, Jackson and Alice are perfect names for them."

"I think so too. And with the children they'll have, they'll have an entire kingdom."

She giggled. "That they will." She stood up. "You play with the kittens for a moment. I'm going to go make the gravy for supper."

"It smells delicious, by the way," he called as she disappeared from his view.

Keri couldn't help but smile at that. He was always making her feel good about what she did. It was nice to have him there supporting her. "Thank you!"

Before the gravy was finished, Harry came back inside, immediately looking for the kittens, and seeming surprised to find them on Mr. Walters's lap. "Are you in charge of the kittens?"

Mr. Walters laughed. "For as long as it takes your wife to make the gravy for our supper!"

Harry hurried into the kitchen to wash his hands before returning to the dining room where the kittens were. "Have you named them yet?" he called to Keri.

"The white one is Jack and the black and white one is Allie."

"Those are nice names."

Mr. Walters smiled. "Short for Jackson and Alice."

Harry thought for a moment, and then he understood, smiling and nodding. "Beautiful names. I'm sure they'll start their own cat empire."

"I was thinking kingdom, but empire will work as well."

Harry was surprised at just how proud the older man looked to have a couple of kittens named after him and his wife. "The names are perfect then, aren't they?"

"I think so," Mr. Walters said, softly stroking one kitten with his finger.

After supper, Harry and Mr. Walters talked for a bit, and they finally decided on the right price for Mr. Walters's land. "It does seem strange to me that it'll be a ranch and not a farm, though."

Harry smiled. "It'll be treated right. That's what really matters, isn't it?"

Mr. Walters nodded. "Thanks for working with this old man til we got to a price we could both agree to."

"I think the world of you, Mr. Walters. I'm happy you've started spending time with us, and sharing your insight."

Keri walked into the room then, noticing that Mr. Walters was beaming with pride. The man needed to know he was appreciated and respected, and they had shown him that in the past week.

Instead of sitting in one of the chairs to talk to the men, she plopped herself down onto the floor to play with the kittens. Perhaps it wasn't the most ladylike thing she could have done, but she did enjoy the babies.

They chased after the string she dangled for them making her laugh, and finally, when they were too tired to keep playing with her, they curled up in her lap and fell asleep. She stroked them each from between the eyes down the bridge of their noses, and their purrs made her feel as if she'd accomplished something truly special that day.

"Your wife wrote a wonderful book," Mr. Walters said.

"Is that so?" Harry looked down at Keri sitting with the kittens. "You've already read it?"

"She brought it to me this morning. I'm going to bring my wife's journal from our Oregon Trail trek to her. It was such a hard time for us, but we were one of the few families in our company to not lose a family member. Alice did a good job of talking about the everyday struggles of the women on the Trail. As much as she didn't want to go, my sweet Alice worked hard to keep our family healthy and happy."

"I can't wait to read it. After I finish the series I'm working on, I may just write a book about the Oregon Trail. I hope this one sells well, but if not, I have a plan for the future."

Mr. Walters chuckled. "Just don't make the poor people in your book eat beans as much as we really had to. It was awful. For a while I was afraid they'd start growing out of my ears."

Keri laughed. "I could write a book about just the beans that they ate. Have you thought of it from the beans' point of view? Imagine how awful it would be to be drowned, boiled, chewed, and then digested. Poor beans..."

Harry sighed. "You look at things much differently than the people around you do," he said to Keri.

She shrugged. "It's a gift. I know it is."

"I agree," Mr. Walters said. "Her way of looking at things from a different perspective is what makes her such a good writer. You can feel it in her books."

"I'm going to have to read that book, I think."

"I can get you a copy of the first one I published," she told him, not really wanting him to read the one she'd just written because she knew he wouldn't be happy that she'd kept in the plotline surrounding the wedding night.

"No, he has to read this one. I have a hard time believing you found time to write that whole book since you arrived in Wyoming. I'd think you were a lazy wife, but your house is always in perfect order."

"It helps that I have a husband who picks up after himself all the time. He doesn't wait for me to follow along behind him to tidy up."

"Well, it shows," Mr. Walters said.

Chapter Ten

After walking Mr. Walters home that evening, Harry walked straight to the loose pages of her book. "Do I need to keep these in order?" he asked.

"I have a feeling you won't like it as much as Mr. Walters and Anne do. I don't think you should read it." Keri didn't want to hear his thoughts on the wedding night scenes because he'd already given them.

"Are you writing things that you don't think I'll like?" he asked, looking perplexed. "Why would you do that?"

She sighed. "You know how you didn't like my idea for many different wedding night scenes that are constantly interrupted? That's what I wrote."

He frowned for a moment, thinking about it. "And you wrote it thinking I would be displeased?"

She nodded. "But Anne and Mr. Walters both loved it and said the way I did it wasn't offensive in any way. I know I should have gotten your approval, and I hope you won't stay angry."

He took a deep breath. "You were a writer before you married me. At first, I didn't understand just how much you felt the need to write. It's almost like a compulsion with you. I haven't been very kind about it."

"I don't want you to be angry, but I have to be true to myself."

"Let me read it, and I'll tell you what I think when I'm done."

She nodded, moving to get some of the fabric she'd purchased for the tablecloth and windows. "I'll sew while you read."

She cut out a small pillow from the fabric and started stitching it together. Every few minutes she'd look up to see if he was angry, but his face always held only amusement.

It was the first night she'd known him to stay up past dark, and he kept reading until he finished the last page. By that time, she'd finished the pillow for the kittens. She'd have to save feathers up, but she could easily do that. She wanted them to have a place of their own.

When Harry finished reading, he carefully stacked the book, making certain all the pages were in order. "I loved it. To me what you wrote was different than what you described to me. Besides, when it comes to writing, you're the professional. I don't even read all that much. You have the right to put whatever you want into your books."

She pursed her lips for a moment as she thought about his words. "Would you be angry if I used my real name and not my pseudonym?"

"Not at all. There's nothing about this book that I would be embarrassed for people to know my wife wrote. You talked about wedding nights in the most general way possible. They never kissed more than once before he was off to take care of the next disaster. I love how he started a ranch at the end so she wouldn't always be worried about him."

"Really?" Keri couldn't believe her ears. He was truly happy with the book she'd written, and she'd been getting ready to fight with him over it. She had misjudged him terribly. "I'm sorry I didn't believe you would support me."

He shook his head. "I don't care what you do, I will always support you. I love you so much, and I'm blessed to be here married to you. I know God was watching out for me as he sent you to me."

Her face lit up. She'd not expected him to say that to her until they were at least Mr. Walters's age. "I love you too," Keri told him. "When I get up during the night to write, it's not because I don't want to be in bed with you. I think I've shown you time and again that I do want to be in bed with you as often as possible. But when I get up it's because I can't sleep. There's some kind of block in my head. If I don't let the words come out and onto paper, then I don't sleep, and when I don't sleep, I get very crabby. I become difficult to live with. So, when it bothers you when I get up and write during the night, I think it's bad for our marriage."

"I can understand that," he said. "I'm not going to complain if you get up during the night anymore. Now that I've read your work, I know that this world needs it. We all need a way to laugh at the end of a long day, and you can make that happen with your writing. I provide meat to people, and you make them laugh. Put together, we're a dinner show!"

Keri laughed. "We're Harry Keri, and the dinner shows start here!"

He took her hand and led her into the parlor, well aware that the kittens were running along behind them, trying to keep up. He sat down on the sofa, and pulled her down beside him, his arm going around her shoulders. "Never be afraid to talk to me," he said. "I hate that you were worried about letting me read your book, and I could see in your face that you were afraid the entire time. There was no need. I made a suggestion, and you didn't take it to heart, but knowing so much more about what sells in books than I do makes it all right if you don't listen."

She nodded. "I will try to be more open about things that worry me." She felt rather than saw one of the kittens scaling the front of her skirt to join them on the sofa. "Well, hello, Allie. Are you needing some love?" She picked the kitten up and gathered it in front of her, happy to hold it close. "Thank you for the kittens. Have I said that yet?"

"I know you love the little critters." He reached down and picked up Jack, who had started climbing his pantleg, his tiny nails digging into Harry's flesh through the fabric. "You don't like being left out, do you, Jack?"

Jack jumped from his lap straight to Keri's and batted Allie in the head. The two of them rolled off her lap onto the floor, still biting and hitting one another. "Should we stop them?" Harry asked, having not really been around kittens.

"No. That's how they play and how they learn to be the ferocious predators they're destined to be."

He chuckled. "Just so they keep the mice at bay."

"They will, and it won't take them long." Keri grinned as they rolled over her foot.

"Does that mean we don't need to feed them?" he asked.

She shook her head. "No, we need to feed them. They'll hunt better on full tummies."

"That makes sense," he said. "I had no idea they would make you so happy!"

"Of course, they make me happy. I may have to write a children's book about the life of a kitten," she said.

"We can hire someone to keep the house so you'll have more time to write," he suggested. "I wouldn't mind at all."

"Maybe after the children start coming," she said. "For now, I like that it's just the two of us living here, and I have no trouble keeping up at all."

"All right. Just know that we don't need the money from your writing, but we also have the means to hire someone if that's what you end up wanting to do."

"I appreciate that." She snuggled into him, her head on his shoulder. "I love it here. I have work to do every day, but it's not difficult work, and there's still time for me to write and spend time with my friend. I had no idea I'd end up married to such a good man."

"It almost felt like we were playing a game of chance, didn't it? It was just chance that brought you here to be my wife. And then chance that made me your husband. Thank God for chance."

She smiled at that. "I can't imagine a happier moment in my life than this one right now."

As they went to bed, they shut the door, settling the kittens first in the dining room. They left one of the windows open so the kittens could get in and out as necessary, but she was sure they'd come back. Even kittens could feel when they lived in a place full of love.

Epilogue

Keri held the baby on her hip as she hurried to the door. A crate was being unloaded from a big wagon full of deliveries. It must be her books.

She did her best not to squeal like a small child, as she was now a mother with a baby of her own. Why, even Allie was a mother now, dealing with her small litter of kittens on her own. For now, they could keep them all at the ranch, but with a few more litters, they would have to give some to others.

"Where do you want it?" the man asked, carrying the huge crate.

Keri held the door open. "On the floor is just fine."

"What do you have in here? Books?"

"Actually yes. It's my newest book."

"Makes sense," the man said. "I got something else for you too." He walked back to the wagon and unpacked a smaller box, which he placed on the table. "This one has a letter attached."

"Thank you so much!"

The man nodded as he hurried back to his wagon and drove away.

Keri looked at the second box, perplexed. Finally, she got a hammer and pried the lid from the crate and looked inside. "A typewriter!" There would be no more hand cramps as she wrote late into the night. Instead, she'd be tapping away at the typewriter. It even had a picture of where each finger should go. She'd learn fast enough, and then all of her manuscripts would be typed before she sent them away.

She put the baby down on his blanket on the floor as she went to the second crate with the hammer. She knew what was inside this one, and it was something she'd been waiting for a long time. Her second book was finally coming out in just a week, and these were her advanced copies.

Prying the lid off the crate, she picked up the first of the books and sniffed deeply. She loved the smell of brand-new books.

Sitting down, she immediately autographed two of the books, planning to give one to Mr. Walters, who was coming for supper that night, and she would take the other to church on Sunday to give to Anne, her dearest friend.

Never in her life had she dreamed she would have a friend like Anne, but she thanked God for the other woman every day.

After feeding her six-month-old son, Albert, she put him down for his nap. They'd debated calling the baby Larry, or Jerry, or even Terry, but had decided he should have a name that was his own, and not just like his parents.

When she moved back to the table, she signed one more book, this time to her mother. Since Albert had been born, she'd appreciated what her mother had done for her a bit more, and she'd worked to keep up a correspondence with her.

Dearest Mother,

I hope this letter finds you in good health and high spirits. The cool winds of autumn have begun to whisper through the vast expanses of Wyoming, painting the landscape with hues of gold and amber. It's a sight that never fails to stir my soul, reminding me of the extraordinary journey that brought me here.

Harry and the baby are well. Our humble home is filled with laughter and love, each day bringing its own unique joys and challenges. The baby is growing like a weed, and I do hope you will get to meet sweet Albert before too terribly long. I see so much of you in him. His eyes are that special shade of blue that I always admired about yours.

Now, I bear exciting news that fills my heart with immense pride and joy. My second book has found its way into the world, a novel born from the depths of my experiences and dreams. It tells the story of a woman who, like me, ventured west as a mail-order bride and discovered a love profound and transformative.

The heroine of my story, much like myself, embarks on a journey driven by hope and courage. She leaves behind everything familiar, venturing into the unknown with a dream of love and belonging. Along the way, she encounters trials and tribulations—each funnier than the last, and each challenge shapes her, molding her into a woman of strength and determination.

Through her journey, she discovers not just the love of a good man but also the love for herself and the life she has chosen. She falls for his children before she falls for him, but I think that's how it is when a woman jumps into motherhood so unexpectedly. Just like me, the heroine finds her place in the untamed beauty of the West.

Mother, I believe this book is a testament to every woman who has dared to dream, to hope, to love. I wish I could hand you the first copy myself, but I am sending it along with this letter. I hope it brings you as much joy as it brought me while writing it.

Every word in this book is a testament to the strength you instilled in me, the courage you nurtured, and the love you showed me. I am who I am because of you. And for that, I am forever grateful.

I look forward to hearing your thoughts on the book. Until then, know that you are in my thoughts and prayers always.

With all my love,

Keri

After finishing her letter, she tucked it into the book she'd signed for her mother and decided she would send it with Harry when he went to town to get her more jars for canning after lunch that day. He could post it, and with the wonder of the modern mail, her mother would have it in her hands in less than a month. What a joy that would be for her to receive.

She looked down at Allie who was looking for some food, and scratched the cat behind her ears. In the year and a half Keri had been in Wyoming, she'd grown into a more well-rounded woman, who loved her family with everything inside her.

Though, now that she had a typewriter, she really must take Harry up on his offer to get a housekeeper. The baby kept her busy enough, and she had another book that must be written. Her fourth in the series was due at her publisher in just three months. It was time for her to get started, and with a loving glance at her new typewriter, she knew it would happen soon.

Milton Keynes UK
Ingram Content Group UK Ltd.
UKHW010935221123
433051UK00001B/79

At the core of Sexy Fruit is a celebration of the dark and light seeds of sensuality, the body, and desire. These are poems that will possess you.

- Annemarie Ní Churreáin, author of *BLOODROOT* (Doire Press, 2017)

Sexy Fruit is full of a kaleidoscopic colourful landscape of poems by Alice Kinsella. "Spain is hot with colour", "pink is the colour of life" and Moore Street is brought alive by strawberries. This collection is full of flesh; the body; mind and nectarines. Kinsella at times meanders with her beautiful language scape, meandering our imagination out of the dull and mundane, evoking senses and bringing them to life, she is perfectly on target. These poems are brave and beautiful.

- Elaine Feeney, author of *RISE* (Salmon Poetry, 2016)

The poems included here are spirited disclosures, ready to come to the threshold of the surreal but also intimate and present in language... The speaker, as in the poems in Flower Press, insists on a charged private space, with every intent of persuading the reader to join her there.

- Eavan Boland, *Poetry Ireland Review*

Published 2018,
Broken Sleep Books:
Talgarreg, Ceredigion, Wales

brokensleepbooks.com

First Edition

Lay out your unrest.

Publisher/Editor: Aaron Kent
Editor: Charlie Baylis

Typeset in UK by Aaron Kent

Broken Sleep Books is committed to
a sustainable future for our planet,
and therefore uses print on
demand publication.

brokensleepbooks@gmail.com

ISBN: 9781724187987

ALICE KINSELLA

Sexy Fruit

Broken Sleep Books
brokensleepbooks.com

Contents

Like everything, this book is
dedicated to M, D, and B.

SEXY FRUIT

It's all sex and fruit, you should
call your book sexy fruit.
– my mum

Hot Tub Hurricane

The storm is coming
    she's on
her way
    from the South West and

the leaves are warning
    us with their frantic desire to

lower into
    the deep heat
        of the foaming
    Jacuzzi
on the deck outside the (4 star) hotel
luxury won't wait but I'm

    staring at the sky
at the leaves
    that are quivering

that are desperate to escape
    the branches on their own terms
before the chaotic battering comes like

        the man beside me all
    muscles and romance

Ophelia they're calling her

O
    Oh
        Ohh
I'm feelin' ya

but I can't stop
    looking at the leaves
        as they're falling

onto my shoulders
onto the heat
of my skin which is steaming
to join the mist that is fleeing
The storm
into the hot tub
whipped into the storm of the chlorine

let's go to the room where there's champagne
and warmth
and
and

I can't stop watching
the leaves

Mea Culpa

Alleyway that ran between estates,
October moon out on full show,
beaming her smiles at us.

Cleaving of something within,
taste of vodka on breath —
white heat — a new burning.

The rust water running in the toilet bowl
and everyone asking where we'd been.
He kept his hands in his pockets.

First frost of a new year, same old moon,
sitting in the playground doing multiplication
in my head, thinking *It's my own stupid fault.*

The shivering shadow of my feet as I swung higher
than I ever had done when parents were watching.

(I don't know how to eat) postcolonial pomegranate

For all of my dealing with J-stor and Greek mythology,
no one ever taught me how to evict the flesh,
polished stones being served for high tea.

I'm not sure it is the seeds, which in other fruit
are spat on the pavement, into tissues,
planted in the ground, that provide
the morning's bittersweetness.

To the poets they look like metaphors,
to you they look like jewels, luxury.

But to me,
—as I pierce each individually with provided cocktail stick
(the kind sharp enough to illicit mother's warning
it's all fun and games until…) —
they look like eyes. A staring pit, a juicy tear.

The seeds I dig out
spit red into my face,
a child coughing blood, a bitten tongue.

If I don't bite down like teeth on bone, but swallow whole,
what inside my belly will grow and grow and grow?

Your name was Edith

In the *Midrash* your name is Edith,
but in Christian tradition they prefer
you nameless, and mute.

I learned to call you Lot's Wife,
the woman following the legacy of temptation.

Sodom, the Eden of the lecherous,
hedonists. Home.

Why did you look back?

Were you afraid your daughters
had fallen behind? Or did you
question the logic of blind faith?

You were forced to abandon
your home, and with it your name,
leaving you with only your choice.

Was there ever a difference
between Eden and Sodom?
You died for your doubt.

I must look back.
I must not fear
the fire I will find there.

If they want me to be salt
I will welcome the rain,
dissolve into oceans.

Colours in Spain

Spain is hot with colour.
Oranges hang in every tree
on Rue de García Barbón,
perfect orbs, like yolks colouring in a pan,
quivering with heat until they bubble, pop, still.
The heat makes everything orange.
I can hear Granddad saying,
You could fry an egg on that pavement,
the kind of burning underfoot, singeing of soles,
reminding you that you, too, are meat –
if it were too hot you would pop
blister like an egg yolk.
You too would fill the air with the smell of luxury.

Cooking Chicken

Pink is the colour of life
of new babies' wet heads
and open screaming mouths.

Pink is the rose hip of a woman at the heart
of what's between her hips
and the tip of my tongue between bud lips.

There's the hint of pink on daisies
when they open their petals to say
hello to the birth of a new day.

But pink is also the colour of death
as the knife slides into flesh
and separates meat into food.

Pink suggests sickness when I pierce the skin,
dissect the sinews, glimpse the tint of it and turn
it to the heat to kill the possibility.

It's the quiver of the comb atop feathers,
and the neck as it's sliced from the body
by the executioner's axe.

It's the colour of cunt
and the hint in the sky
when the cock crows.

Strawberries

I buy them fresh on Moore Street
for less than I thought
such luxury commanded.

Displayed in plastic cartons mismatch
of sizes and shapes, all carefully balanced
to create empty space

while leaving the illusion of red,
and fresh fruit, and wet tongues,
champagne glasses, and golden rings.

At home, I take a knife, the sharpest
silver glint, in which I can see
my own shine of teeth and strawberry lips.

Yank green heads
like hair from a follicle
until what's left behind
bleeds, oozes, overflows.

Under my nails now, rivers
through the creases on my hands,
dyeing me pink, or pinker.

Slice the freckled skin to see the centre
mottled pink and white and red,
in the heart of it a hollow

like the atrium I pawed open
in school, the sheep's organ
splayed, cut cross ways in my hands.

Careful, then, not to lick my fingers
the blood thickened black,
dyed me red, or redder.

I stroke the curve of the strawberry
as I split it with my fingers.
Licking its excess.

Lips and fingers bloodied red now,
just like then, colouring me shades
of dawn inside and out.

Carrot / Stick

Inside the nightclub is red.
It sweats light onto bare
bodies. The salt, the music.

There's a wooden cross
and you're tied to it, Christ-like.
But you are no martyr,
you drive the nails in yourself.

In the corner a fat man is being sucked off
by a girl of no more than nineteen.
He's a doctor. His belly flops onto her nose.

An adult boy is curled up in a cage.
His mistress uses her size nine stilettos
to prick pits in his pillow bum.

The belt burns red rivulets
into your cream clean skin.

As we approach the unbearable
we discover there's nothing to fear.

In places like this I am a child

A CCTV camera watches the baptismal font. I swirl my
hands through the water, make faces at the lens. I enter the
confessional box on the priest's side, flick on the red light to
say occupied. Who thought of it first, priests or prostitutes?
In the mesh, between my box and the sinner's, someone has
cut out a hole. A perfect circle. *Glory hole,* I say,
accidentally, out loud. I think of my friend that had the
affair with the priest he met on Grindr. How he'd suck his
cock in the confessional box, and make jokes about the
leather padding on the kneelers. I turn the crucifix
upside-down for no reason.
Maybe I am making up for lost childhoods.

In the graveyard a headstone has been placed in the hollow
of the birch. The bark has begun to envelop the stone. The
wind tears through the top branches and it sounds like tidal
waves.
Before I finish writing this poem it starts raining. Let's call it
an act of God.

Ultrasound

The Eccles Street Park is closed to the public,
gates chained protecting empty paths and benches.
In the orb of metal, *Healing Hands* hold flame.
An apple tree, the only one, has lost its fruit to the month.

In the waiting room of the breast health clinic
eyebrows sink as faces collapse slowly,
each ticking minute pulling heavy on every line.

October sun, low hanging already at three o clock,
catches the fire flicker of the leaves, sets them alight.
I can see every vein within,
lines holding strong as the blade decays.

In the stained glass window,
– sky high blue and red –
a crown washed in sun promises
Our Lady will have mercy.

I thought the first time would be a heartbeat,
not circles within circles – black holes.

The apples gather in their dozens at the roots.
Every one is brown, gold, rotting.
So many perfect apples.

Garden of Angels

Across the lake roll the echoes
of children playing.

The carcass of Moore Hall still stands
on the hill overlooking Lough Carra.

In the woods, the little that remains
of life lies buried,

a raised tomb to remember: George Moore and family,
and behind that, a garden.

A scattering of rocks break through ivy.
Whitewashed crosses glow like the star stickers

on the ceiling of my childhood bedroom.
No pen has marked these uncarved stones

that lie as if fallen from farm walls.
Where babies too young for heaven

were planted like bulbs,
the air quivers with the ghosts of mothers

laying new life into dead earth,
unable to put loss into words.

Fertility tests

(Mayo General, January 2018)

The doctor outside the gynae ward leans against the wall,
says to his friend *it doesn't matter*
if it's the size of a pea or a golf ball
kidney stones are
the worst pain imaginable.

You can't make this shit up.

The Virgin is perching
in her newly renovated niche.
She won't look me in the eye.

The stone-faced doctor ticks boxes,
asks if I'm sexually active,
if I'm on the contraceptive pill.
Yes, No.
You are married then?

A nurse appears with a needle
to take bloods. I say
No. Not today.
She makes a barrier of herself,
bruises my arm with comfort,
doesn't listen to *phobia,*
or *I'm not fucking joking,*
points to the sign about not tolerating
aggression from patients.

Impaled on the ultrasound wand
I'm thinking of Excalibur
and destiny.
The doctor looking at the screen
says everything is as it should be.

On finding my first grey hair at 24

I'm bleeding for the first time in six months.

This year I've lost a stone and put on two. My body keeps reminding me of itself: *You can't do this without me.*

My friend says her daughter keeps growing more beautiful, while she can feel herself wilting, but this doesn't make her sad like it should.

I am editing my first book and afraid I'll start calling it my baby.

A boy that wants to fuck me told me people only pretend to be happily married.

The man I loved asked too many questions. We separated amicably.

The title is a lie. This is my third grey hair.

I pluck it out, paint my lips labia red.

Supersweet Yellow Flesh Nectarine

Beat me up internally until I'm blue
as berries crushed in the Nutri-blender
and inked over bowls of porridge

first thing in the morning
when I'm writing in the box room
and you're writing in the kitchen.

Bite me like a still pink plum
putting up a fight
feel my softness yield to your teeth.

SUPERSWEET YELLOW FLESH NECTARINES
says the sticker when I'm shopping
because nothing is as sexy as domesticity.

Crack me like a coconut
as you splash milk into the pot.
Prise me open like a monkey might.

Press me to a pulp,
lick me off your fingers,
drink me like you're dying.

Feel me bubble on your tongue,
effervescing like Prosecco.
Squeeze me so I pop and our cups overflow.

Peach, on beach

Each bite smashes like a foot on broken glass.
In the chambers of my ears, crunching,
while the outer cup of my ear sucks in sea.
Crash, crash, crash. The slap of the waves
as wet as my tongue burying into this peach.

Women are scattered along the beach like seals,
sinking their bodies into the sand.
Brown nipples, downy breasts, the dip
and mound of bellies, rising and falling and rising.

The noon sun has no mercy on my skin,
turning white to pink. I am not protected
like the fuzz of my peach, though I tear
through that with more force than the sun.
I wriggle my tongue to the stone heart
like an urgent worm.

I find no pulse of life, yet it is flesh:
not forbidden, but made for me.
God did not throw manna over the edge of his cloud.
He threw peaches, wet gold falling like raindrops full of sun.

Soft fists of light, giving way to my lips.
Squat, puffy, begging for my blushes.
They make me want to undress, expose
the peach of my skin to the sun,
not care if it burns.

Eve

If there were a universal mother,
she wouldn't be some painted virgin
unwilling to accept a woman's boiling blood.

She could only be the woman
who saw pleasure and wisdom,
and took them,

questioned the commands of the father
taught the man how to desire.

She knew that the secret to life
is to taste it,
in all its sinful glory.

Don't listen to what they tell you.
She didn't regret it.

When

after If- by Rudyard Kipling

When you can say the words that are not listened to,
But keep on saying them because you know they're true.
When you can trust each other when all men doubt you,
And from support of other women make old words new.
When you can wait, and know you'll keep on waiting,
That you'll be lied to, but not sink to telling lies.
When you know you may hate, but not be consumed by hating,
And know that beauty doesn't contradict the wise.

When you can dream – and know you have no master.
When you can think – let those thoughts drive your aim.
When you receive desire and abuse from some Bastard
And treat both manipulations just the same.
When you hear every trembling word you've spoken
Retold as lies, from a dishonest heart.
When you have had your life, your body, broken
But stop, breathe, and rebuild yourself right from the start.

When you can move on but not forget your beginnings,
And do what's right no matter what the cost,
Lose all you've worked for, forget the aim of winning
And learn to find the victory in your loss.
When you can see every woman struggle to
Create a legacy, for after they are gone,
And work with them, when nothing else connects you
Except the fight in you which says: 'Hold on!'

When you can feel the weight of life within you
But know that you alone are just enough.
When you know not to judge on some myth of virtue
To be discerning, but not too tough.
When you know that you have to fight for every daughter
Even though you are all equal to any son.
When you know this, but still fill your days with laughter
You'll have the earth, because you are a woman!

Water women

I. *Tobernalt holy well*

Ribbons braided round branches like plaits.
Nothing grows on this tree.

Mary, Jesus, various kneeling saints encased in concrete,
sprouting Stations of the Cross look like a pet cemetery.

And the women,

with their house coats and rosary beads,
light candles that flicker through the leaves

like a city in the distance.

And the water

trips down the hillside, between roots and statues,
pools itself into a well, where a sign has been hung saying

please don't throw coins in the water

The women come anyway,
with their wishes.

The women who's faces are tired
from praying for those they've outlived.

II. Dead Man's Point

In the summer you can't move for young ones, they'll rob
the car keys from your shoes while you're swimming.

But now it is Spring, the water is colder than cold.
The tide runs from the setting of sun, fills the pool.

Whether used or not. Walls, could be Eastern bloc,
take mouthfuls of saltwater. Eroding stone. Rot.

And the women have come in their cars.
They are smoking with the windows rolled up.

Headlamps look the sun straight in the eye.
Young women in puffy jackets, bleached hair,

mascara halfway down to their tits, parked apart
from each other, all facing the water.

Blood stone

In Ballinskelligs I read the names.
Our own, my mother's on her father's side.

The stone wall standing since the twelfth century,
though the fossils embedded, like tire tracks
in mud, show an unwritten history.

A spider web, hours old, spun into a crumbling nook,
traps drops of drizzle like spit.

I climb the curve of Bolus Head
as the sun drops, the rocks
make silhouettes, shadow puppets.

Too high to hear the waves,
just the ghostly hiss of mist.

At the turn of the peak, crows line up in pairs,
the shuffle of their wings, loud as clapping,
bring superstition and a shot of cortisol.

I slip, crack my knee on a rock.
The skin holds in blood
crushed to the colour of stone.

Acknowledgments

First and foremost thanks to Aaron Kent and Charlie Baylis for your hard work and encouragement.

Thanks and acknowledgments are due to the editors of the following publications, where some of these poems have appeared: *Banshee, Live Encounters, Poethead, Poetry Ireland Review, Skylight 47, The Irish Times, The North, The Pickled Body,* and *The Rochford Street Review.*

For their support I would like to thank Books Upstairs, Listowel Writers' Week, Cill Rialaig Artists' Residency, Over the Edge, Offaly County Council, Poetry Ireland, and Dublin UNESCO City of Literature.

Thank you to Alvy Carragher, Ingrid Casey, Lisa Frank, Dani Gill, Seanín Hughes, Ruth McKee, Kerrie O' Brien, Liz Quirke, Anne Tannam, and to Mary O'Donnell and the staff and students of the MA in Writing 2018 at NUI Galway.

Special thanks to Jessica Traynor, Eavan Boland, Annemarie Ní Chuireáin, and Elaine Feeney.

Love and constant thanks to Éadaoin, Paul, and Brian.

LAY OUT YOUR UNREST

Printed in Great Britain
by Amazon